The Wandering Mind

The Wandering Mind

A book of short stories

Syed Ibrahim Rizvi

GenNext Publication

Published by

GenNext Publication
5, Ansari Road
Daryaganj, New Delhi-110002
Phone: 011-47034999, 9811692060

E-mail: gennextpublication@hotmail.com

Distribution Network
gyanbooks.com
India, USA, Canada, UK, Australia, France

ISBN: 978-93-5663-173-1 (PB)

First Published, 2024

Printed at: Gyan Press, Delhi.

The Wandering Mind
Author: Syed Ibrahim Rizvi

Dedication

This book is dedicated to my father
Late Agha Rizvi
who through his genes gave me the gift of
weaving thoughts into words

Contents

Preface

Scientists attribute the higher cognitive abilities of Homo sapiens as the main reason why humans have been able to become masters of this world. As human evolution progressed the most important change witnessed was in the networking of the brain which created an attribute we now recognize as Intelligence. Despite having no obvious physical attributes, humans because of their intelligence have been able to outnumber and outclass all big animals. The higher intelligence of Homo sapiens also bestowed humans with a range of emotions. No other animal displays the array of emotions which humans experience. Another great feature of humans is their ability to create fictional thoughts which enable them to delve into the past, live in the present and think about the future.

The creation of fictional thought is an attribute which has made human life so colourful. The human mind is capable of experiencing emotions even in the virtual domain. The art of creating fictional stories have played a pivotal role all throughout the 2,00,000 years of the history of Homo sapiens. Fictional thought, in the form of stories, is universal and prevalent in all cultures and geographical regions of the world. The compilation of such human feelings laced with beautiful emotions constitutes a very important pillar of human existence and is known as Literature.

The present book is a compilation of seven short stories which provide a glimpse of most human emotions including love, romance, empathy, belief, sorrow, joy and jealousy. The book would make an interesting companion for an audience with an interest in the English language.

Syed Ibrahim Rizvi

ACKNOWLEDGEMENT

My first book '**A Kaleidoscope of Thoughts**' published in 2020, the second book '**A Tryst with Emotions**' published in 2022 and the third '**Hues of Life'** published in 2023 have been very well received by the audience. People from all walks of life and well-wishers congratulated and encouraged me to continue my journey into literature. I acknowledge all my peers who have been eloquent in their praise and criticism for my short stories. I would be failing in my duty if I do not acknowledge the dedicated teachers of my first school, the Boys High School, Allahabad, who took pains to instill in me the subtlety of English language.

Syed Ibrahim Rizvi

Someone Else's Bride

From his seat in the classroom, Jamal could see his new Hero Splendor parked outside on the road, in fact, today morning he had parked his bike deliberately at a vantage point so that it could be visible from the classroom. The Professor was teaching something about Artificial Intelligence, but Jamal's mind was more rivetted to the new bike which his parents had gifted him yesterday. Jamal glanced at his watch, he made a mental calculation, the class would probably be over in ten minutes.

After the class, as Jamal approached his motorcycle, someone called from behind. Jamal realised this was Rashid his two years junior in the B Tech course. Rashid lived close to Jamal's house. As Jamal looked back, Rashid took hasty steps and requested whether he can pillion ride with Jamal back home. The happy look on Jamal's face was inviting enough for Rashid to sit on the motorcycle. The way Jamal started the motorcycle and his sudden acceleration was a tell-tale sign of someone trying to advertise his new motorcycle. Raising a small ball of dust, Jamal veered his motorcycle towards the exit gate of the college.

Despite heavy traffic, Jamal found the journey of nine kilometers back home pleasurable. Today he didn't curse the cyclists and autorickshaw drivers who crossed his path taking unexpected turns. Rashid sat on the pillion seat; he had no inkling of the emotions of his senior who was driving this motorcycle. Oblivious of Jamal's thoughts, Rashid looked forward to reaching his home. Noorullah road was, as always, heavy with traffic. Even Jamal had to slow down his motorcycle.

While Jamal navigated between the maze of autorickshaws and two wheelers, Rashid's eyes caught a sight which to his eyes was indeed a sight to behold. At the intersection of the side lane, stood an utterly beautiful girl in *' head scarf'* haggling with a rikshaw driver. Even in this attire, she looked like a princess. Rashid's heart skipped a beat. A rush of sudden adrenaline overwhelmed his physiology. His eyes refused to lose sight of this attractive face. Now it was Jamal's turn of being oblivious of how dazed Rashid was while sitting on the pillion seat, dumbstruck with the beauty of this unknown girl. As soon as the obstruction cleared, Jamal accelerated his motorcycle and Rashid lost his lovely damsel.

Jamal dropped Rashid at a corner which was close to his house and raced to his own house. His mother and sister were standing at the gate, purposely waiting for Jamal. A beaming Jamal pushed his motorcycle, with a care befitting the entry of a new bride, inside the gate.

Rashid knocked at his house but didn't notice who opened the door. His mind was still burdened with the memory of that ethereal beauty. He quietly went to his room. As evening faded into night, the lingering thought of the beautiful girl continued to haunt Rashid. Night came and brought sleep but Rashid continued to dream. The next morning Rashid started conjuring thoughts of finding the whereabouts of the girl.

It was around four in the evening when Rashid reached the intersection of Noorullah road where he had seen the beautiful girl yesterday. The intersection was crowded. Roadside sweet meat shops were doing brisk business. A fruit seller advertised his collection of fruits in a professional voice without giving a thought whether anyone was listening or not. Rashid realised the fruit seller was taking the names of even some fruits which were not present on the cart. Rashid concluded that this fruit seller was yelling as a habit, a routine he had been following for decades. While the evening was playing out in this busy intersection, Rashid's eyes scanned the nearby lane for something which was akin to finding a needle in the haystack.

Rashid stood aimlessly in a corner; every veiled girl that passed his sight gave a ray of hope. Every hijab clad face flattered to deceive. Rashid's thoughts were broken by the sudden blaring of the *'azaan'* from the mosque on the opposite side of the intersection. He realised this was *'maghrib'* time. It was already getting dark. Rashid felt heavy at heart and started walking back home.

Rashid found it hard to sleep that night. Paradoxically the fleeting memory of that girl in *'hijab'* was not fading with time. Rashid lost count of time that night, finally he dozed off.

Feigning health issues Rashid did not go to college the next day although at around three in the afternoon he found an excuse to venture out of the house. He spent approximately three hours at the spot where he had seen the girl two days back. At the stroke of '*azaan*' Rashid walked trudging back to his house.

It was the fourth day; Rashid again went to the Noorullah road trisection more as a habit and without any real intent. In the last four days his mind had already convinced him that finding the girl was almost impossible. Rashid found an empty stool at the roadside tea stall and ordered a tea. It was almost at the stroke when he had the first sip that a rikshaw stopped in front of him. The passenger was a girl wearing a sequined green dress. Rashid saw the face when the passenger alighted from the rikshaw. His heart missed not one but two beats. The beauty of the face was unmistakably true to his memory. *Voila* he had found the girl!!

The girl paid the rikshaw driver, adjusted her hijab and took the lane walking in measured steps. Rashid discarded the tea and walked towards the girl. After approximately fifty yards the girl stopped at a door, she pressed a bell and went inside as the door opened. Rashid kept walking. He passed the door and stole a glimpse of the house. With a spring in his stride, that evening Rashid didn't wait for the *'azaan'*, he returned to his house.

An innately feminine instinct prompted Zeba that someone was following her while she walked fifty paces to her house after alighting from the rikshaw. While she was closing the door from inside, she had seen a young man pass in front of her house. She observed that the young man was hesitant when he had turned his head to see the door close. From inside the small crack in the door, Zeba could see the face of the man. The face sported an apprehensive innocence. Zeba found this look endearing.

From the fifth day onwards, Rashid had found his spot. On an average he would invariably catch the sight of the girl once every alternate day. He would walk a few paces behind the girl while she would traverse the fifty yards to her house. Zeba knew that she was being followed by someone but she never felt stalked. The young man had always maintained an amicable distance which was trustworthy.

After a few weeks it had become a routine for Rashid to enjoy the company of the girl for a few seconds, albeit from a distance. For Zeba this was also a new experience. Her strict middle-class upbringing had never allowed her to even think of looking at someone not related to her. The mere thought of a young man following her respectfully, without any obvious reason, brought some highly pleasant emotions which were hitherto alien to her. She would find reasons to prolong her routine of paying the rikshaw, this provided her the time to seek the young man who would be sitting invariably on the stool beside the tea stall.

Where there is a will, there is a way. It was within three months that Rashid could muster the courage of one day walk alongside the girl and mutter a meek 'hello'. The girl had smiled. This time it was the evolutionary instinct of Rashid to understand that the girl had taken his courageous act in an affable spirit.

Within a fortnight the fifty yards that Rashid walked with Zeba became the most treasured moment for Rashid. What Rashid did not know was that Zeba too looked forward to this interlude. Rashid came to know that Zeba had this year completed her graduation and was now enrolled in a hobby class. In the evening, she went to the hobby center. Rashid told Zeba that he was doing B Tech from a city college. Zeba gave Rashid her phone number on the condition that he would not call her while she was at home. He can only text her.

Zeba found Rashid a perfect gentleman. Rashid on his part maintained a healthy respect for Zeba, he respected her privacy and never asked for any favour which would go against the ingrained values of Zeba's family and culture. Zeba loved the way Rashid talked to her; she specially enjoyed his subtle humour. In free moments Zeba loved to think about Rashid.

Two years had passed from the day when Rashid had first seen Zeba while she stood haggling with the rikshaw driver on the Noorullah road intersection. In the past two years, Rashid had become too dependent on Zeba for emotional support. On her part Zeba found the company of Rashid an emotional stabilizer, she would share with him all her sundry thoughts and bask in Rashid's humour.

Rashid's third year end semester exams were round the corner and to avoid distraction he had switched off his mobile phone for the duration of the examination. Even this he did on the advice of Zeba.

The March evening was pleasantly cool. It was just after dusk that Zeba's house had few visitors which were not known to Zeba's parents. The visitors comprising three women and two men proposed Zeba's marriage to a boy who had a job in a multinational company in Mumbai. They showed Zeba's parents the photograph of the boy.

That evening while Zeba sobbed in her room, her parents deliberated in hushed tones the pros and cons of the proposal. The antecedents of the boy were good. A phone call to a distant cousin in Mumbai confirmed the address where the boy was living. The next day Zeba's parents invited the extended family to dwell upon the proposal. The consensus emerged that the proposal was good. An elder cousin took the initiative to break this news to Zeba. No one gave a thought whether Zeba's concurrence was also required.

While Rashid was busy preparing for his end semester examination he studied till late night. Invariably when he slept, he would dream about Zeba. The mutual decision of being out of contact was painful but also romantically exciting. Tonight, when Rashid slept, he had a frightening dream. He saw Zeba running frantically on a road calling his name. Rashid's sleep got disrupted. He looked at the watch it was two in the night. On an impulse he wanted to text Zeba but then decided against. He gulped a mouthful of water and went back to sleep.

The boy's parents agreed on all the conditions put forth by Zeba's parent but insisted on the date of marriage. At their insistence and much to the discomfort of Zeba's parents, the date was fixed just ten days from the present date. The boy's parents reiterated effusively that they did not want dowry or any gifts. Marriage preparations started in Zeba's home in earnest. A thousand emotions boiled in Zeba's mind but she had no clue how to manage those emotions. She did take the liberty of contacting Rashid but his phone was switched off.

Zeba became someone else's bride even before the time came for Rashid to switch on his phone. As soon as Rashid finished his last paper, he texted Zeba. An undue time lapse of getting a reply prompted Rashid to again text her. Rashid waited for an hour still no reply. In desperation, Rashid did the unthinkable. He dialed Zeba but the message made him even more concerned. Zeba's phone was switched off.

Rashid went to the lane which housed Zeba's house. The remnants of a few pieces of decorative flowers were enough to signal that some function had taken place in this household. Fighting tears, he stopped at the roadside shop and enquired whether there was a function of some sort in the house which he pointed out. The shopkeeper looked at Rashid, in a voice devoid of any emotion he said that it was the marriage of a girl a few days back. Rashid felt heavy at heart. It was at that moment the *muezzin* broke the advent of dusk with the *'azaan'* heralding It was time for the *'maghrib'* prayer.

Loaded with memories of Rashid, Zeba boarded the flight to Mumbai. Deliberately she had switched off her mobile phone. Looking at the phone reminded her of Rashid and she was not sure how she would be able to face Rashid.

Life in Mumbai was very different from the sleepy hometown of her parents. Zeba's husband doted on her. It was another matter that frequently, even when her husband romantically enticed her, Zeba's thoughts meandered to the time spent with Rashid.

Time is a big healer. Evolutionary psychology explains that males are affected more by romantic breakups than females. In some months, Zeba's mind had moved Rashid to a far recess of her brain. Zeba's husband pampered her with love and affection and Zeba responded with devotion. Rashid was no longer an impediment in her thoughts. While Zeba melted in her new role, it was Rashid who found it hard to reconcile to the new normal. Very frequently his thoughts would bring back the memory of Zeba. Rashid became a recluse; he bided his time giving more importance to his B Tech course. In a few months he appeared for his final examinations and surprised everyone by standing first in order of merit. It was an icing on the cake that Rashid got the best job offer during campus selections.

Two years had passed in Zeba's married life, she was happy except for the lingering feeling that she had not been able to conceive. Although two years was not a big time and a cause for worry but she knew that her husband wanted a child. He loved children. In intimate moments he would invariably open up and share his feelings with Zeba. Biological reasons apart, Zeba wanted to conceive to make her husband feel happy. She felt this act would in a way repay her loving husband for all the affection and care he bestowed on her.

Time passed; Zeba continued to live a life of a princess. Affluence had also made her prettier. Her husband adored her. While everything was going fine, Zeba's in-laws now started finding ways to obliquely suggest that it was time the couple thought of a child. Thus, it was in an intimate moment that Zeba suggested to her husband that they should consult a doctor for their inability to conceive. After an appointment the couple visited a renowned clinic after a few days. The doctor suggested a slew of tests for Zeba. It took almost fifteen days for all the tests. To her surprise all the tests came fine. Despite this the doctor prescribed a few medicines for Zeba and the treatment started. Another six months passed with no success. Another appointment was scheduled and both Zeba and her husband visited the doctor again. This time the doctor prescribed a few tests for Zeba's husband.

Other than the latent infertility issue, Zeba couldn't have asked for more in her marriage. And therefore, she became excited when on a Saturday evening her husband announced that he had invited an old acquaintance for dinner this evening. Zeba was fond of cooking and since mid-afternoon she prepared an assortment of dishes for the evening dinner.

As the bell rang, since her husband had just gone to washroom, Zeba went to the door to welcome the guest. As Zeba opened the door she froze. Rashid, looking dapper in the black tuxedo, was standing at the door. Rashid too was stunned. They both looked flummoxed. Without saying a word Zeba gave way and Rashid moved inside the huge drawing room. Memories came flooding for Zeba and Rashid. Both felt utterly hapless to the present circumstance. It was in this moment of doldrum that Zeba's husband Jamal walked in. In an animated gesture he welcomed Rashid hugging him tightly. Facing Zeba he introduced Rashid, saying he was two-year junior to him in college.

While Zeba took leave and hurried inside, Rashid felt a strange unease. He fought his memories while pretending to continue conversation with Jamal. Jamal, intelligent as he was, felt an unusual pause in conversation. While still talking to Rashid, his eighty-six billion neurons tried to fathom the cause of this subtle hesitancy on the part of Zeba. Despite this momentary glitch, the evening went as it was supposed to be. Rashid and Jamal recollected with glee the memories of the day when Rashid had hitch hiked with Jamal the day when Jamal had for the first time took his new Hero Splendor to the college. What Rashid didn't mention was how he had seen Zeba on the Noorullah Road trisection and how beautiful she looked.

That night, Jamal made love to Zeba. As Jamal initiated the intimate moment, he realised that Zeba's mind was not synchronised with the demands of her body. Jamal found this strange. It was a just a fleeting thought and soon Jamal's testosterone overwhelmed his senses. He kissed Zeba and felt exhausted.

That night Rashid felt too confused at the turn of events. His mind debated intensely whether this chance meeting with Zeba was just a coincidence or destiny. That night while his brain refused to sleep, a kaleidoscope of thoughts engulfed his senses. He vividly remembered the time spent with Zeba. The past memories came flooding, his heart ached. Rashid realised the wound of losing Zeba was still raw.

While Jamal caressed Zeba after an insipid romantic session, Zeba's mind travelled far reliving the moments which she had spent with Rashid. For a moment she yearned to talk to Rashid. It was second time that evening that Jamal felt there was a pause in intimacy from Zeba. Already exhausted from the love making session, Jamal debunked this frivolous thought and closed his eyes. He slept soundly.

While Jamal had gone to his office, Zeba continued to rewind the events of the yesterday evening. Despite her firm resolve, strengthened by firm religious upbringing, today Zeba's mind did start a comparison between Jamal and Rashid. The more her mind meandered, the more she could see the beauty of Rashid's endearing personality. The saner part of Zeba's brain coaxed her that such comparison was a sin. To escape such thoughts Zeba started reading the Quran.

Jamal had observed lately that Zeba would frequently be lost in thought. His mind worked hard to find the reason. He pampered Zeba with gifts but his sharp mind could still see a sense of melancholy in Zeba. The continued change in Zeba's behaviour made Jamal a bit apprehensive. It was Sunday and after lunch Jamal preferred a short siesta. While Jamal slept, Zeba silently picked his phone and scrolled the contacts. Way down the list she found 'Rashid'. A thought suddenly prompted Zeba to copy the number. The saner part of her brain did prompt her that this was a sin, but Zeba couldn't resist the urge to copy the number. While she copied, a wrong touch started the call to Rashid but in a fraction of second she stopped the call. No harm done.

As evening progressed and Zeba made tea for a lazy Jamal still in bed, Jamal picked his phone to check messages. Scrolling the calls he observed that he had called Rashid sometime back. Jamal pressured his mind to recollect why he had called Rashid and then realised that he had not made the call. While Zeba brought tea, it was Jamal's turn to go back in thoughts. He understood that while he slept someone had made a call or had searched for Rashid on his phone. While he sipped tea, his intelligent mind was joining the dots between Zeba's strange attitude when Rashid had come to their house for dinner, the abstract change in Zeba's behaviour lately and the fact that Rashid shared the same hometown with Zeba.

In between sinister thoughts, Jamal repeatedly coaxed his mind into believing that his mind was thinking in the wrong direction. It had been a good eight days since he had given samples for the tests which the doctor had prescribed and today, he made it a point to collect the reports. After collecting the reports that evening, he decided to show the reports to the doctor. By chance the doctor was available. After ten minutes when Jamal came out of doctor's chamber, he felt he had aged ten years. The doctor had told him that due to a congenital defect he would not be able to father a child.

Zeba accosted Jamal at the door and looked concerned at Jamal's countenance. Jamal said that he had a hectic day in the office and that everything was fine. While Zeba and Jamal had their evening tea, Jamal's thoughts continued to veer towards his medical report. In between these thoughts, his mind also came up with an image of Rashid. Jamal felt a strange emotion which he had never felt before. Suddenly everything looked meaningless in life.

In the week that followed, Jamal looked sick. Zeba showed concern. She tried to make him happy but Jamal felt lost. That weekend Jamal again invited Rashid for dinner. He again didn't tell Zeba who was coming. Jamal observed Zeba's and Rashid's reaction when they faced each other. Jamal could sense an excitatory warmth in Rashid's countenance when he addressed Zeba in conversation. At the other end, Zeba seemed subdued and tried to avoid direct eye contact with Rashid.

Jamal's condition seemed worse. He ate less and avoided watching cricket which he was fond of. As was the routine, Jamal and

Zeba slept late on Sunday. This Sunday was no exception. When Zeba got up at nine in the morning, she found Jamal still sleeping. Zeba found a strange stillness in Jamal's posture. She poked Jamal to get up. Jamal didn't move. An involuntary shriek came out of Zeba's mouth. She pulled Jamal towards her but the limp body was already cold. The reality dawned. Twenty-five minutes later, the doctor officially pronounced Jamal dead confirming that the cause of death was heart failure.

In the days that followed, a large number of people came for condolence. Rashid also came. He felt sorry for Zeba. Although in that moment of grief Zeba didn't talk to him but Rashid could feel Zeba's loss.

The Jamal household became silent soon. Very few visitors came to console Zeba. It was on the fifth day that Zeba got a call on Jamal's phone. She read the name; it was Rashid. Zeba didn't pick the phone. Again, the next day Zeba received a phone call from Rashid, she ignored. Then she received a text message. The message said '*I want to meet you*'. Reading that message Zeba's thought went back five years, she used to get similar messages. Unknowingly she picked the phone and replied '*Yes*'.

Albeit engrossed in grief, Zeba found the visit of Rashid very refreshing. After five years Rashid was as ebullient as ever. Zeba had the feeling that Rashid was making effort to make her happy. As Rashid took her leave after fifteen minutes, Zeba felt she wanted him to stay a few more minutes.

Unannounced Rashid again visited Zeba a few days later. This time Zeba sported a faint smile while she greeted Rashid. The conversation focused on many topics but both consciously avoided any mention of events of the past. Subsequent to that visit, Rashid came to meet Zeba often. Zeba also looked forward to such visits. It was on one such visit, Rashid offered to take Zeba out for dinner. Zeba refused citing that after the death of her husband, in Islamic law, she was not allowed to leave the home for next ninety days. In his mind Rashid made a rough calculation, it had been forty days since Jamal's sad demise.

Days passed and Zeba became normal. Sometimes she herself called Rashid. In hushed tones, sometimes the womenfolk suggested within themselves that Zeba must marry again. She was too young to lead a life of a widow. A few relatives who were close to Zeba even went to the extent of saying that Rashid could be a suitable candidate.

A few weeks later, while having tea, Rashid asked Zeba abruptly the question which Zeba feared. Rashid asked Zeba why she had left him without telling and had married Jamal. Perhaps Zeba was waiting for an instigation. For ten minutes she sobbed and told the whole story of her marriage to Rashid. It was dark outside and there was no one in the room. Rashid got up and hugged Zeba. Zeba didn't protest. She complemented in Rashid's arms.

Eighty days had passed and Rashid became an everyday visitor to Zeba. Zeba enjoyed his company, she laughed at his jokes. In conversation she had also opened up to going outside with Rashid after the ninety-day period. Rashid knew that this benign statement meant far more than what was mentioned. He felt happy.

It was the eighty-eight day and Zeba was excited. She had made plans to go out with Rashid on a dinner date after two days. In preparation of her new plans Zeba decided to revamp her living room and bedroom. She removed all the items of Jamal and kept them in a bag. As a last preparation, she picked the Photo frame which displayed a photo of Jamal and herself and was about to put that in the bag that she saw a folded envelope pasted on the backside. She took that envelope and opened it. Inside there was a letter addressed to Zeba. Zeba started reading the letter.

Jamal had mentioned in the letter that his death was not a sudden death. He had planned the death to look real. In fact, he had committed suicide by consuming a chemical Isoproterenol which triggers heart failure. He had also mentioned that as per the medical report he would never have become a father and, he felt, that Zeba would be happier with Rashid. He had committed suicide so that he could leave the scene with dignity while Zeba could marry Rashid and have children. Neatly stapled with the letter was another polythene envelope with a white powder bearing a sticker Isoproterenol.

Zeba was stunned. An unending flow of tears trickled down her cheeks. A spate of memories flooded her mind. Zeba felt Jamal was at her side pampering her as always. She realised the phone was ringing. With tears forming a convex coating on her eyes, she saw the name Rashid. She felt no urge to pick the phone.

Rashid found it strange that Zeba would not take her calls. He had come to another city or else would have rushed to Zeba's home. The next day as soon as Rashid reached the city, he didn't go to his home, he rushed to Zeba. The door was open. He ran to the bedroom. Zeba was lying on the bed with both hands clutching a Photo frame which displayed the wedding photo of a beaming Jamal and a resplendent Zeba.

In fifteen minutes, a doctor in measured official tone pronounced that Zeba had died due to heart failure.

A Judicial Dilemma

The premises of the sessions court was as usual abuzz with activity. Lawyers in their black coats moved in hurried steps jostling with the clients, aimless onlookers, lazy police personnel and tea sellers. To someone not tuned to this scene it would seem rather chaotic but to the bustling crowd the situation on this Tuesday morning was as normal as the rising of the sun. The entry of the blue barricaded police van which snaked its way into the premises from the gate also seemed to be a usual sight. The heavy iron mesh on the sides of the vehicle provided a glimpse of the prisoners being brought to the sessions court by the police. A few disinterested police guards accompanied the prisoners. The rear gate of the prison van was opened by one of the guards and the prisoners along with guards trooped out. Some of the onlookers had come closer to the prisoners and talked as if this was a routine affair. While most prisoners looked nonchalant in their countenance a few looked worn out and walked at a pace which belied their age. Among the prisoners alighting from the police van on that Tuesday morning was Manoj. He looked much beyond his forty-five years age, the sunken cheeks and the hollow eyes clearly showed that he was not among the hardened criminals. A pan chewing potbellied police man held Manoj's hand and walked towards the court number three which was at the far end of the long corridor.

Judge Sushil Kumar was a punctual judge. As was his routine he was invariably on his chair by 10.15 am. This morning it was no different. By 11.15 am, he had already heard almost twenty cases. Having been in the judicial position for the last fifteen years he had fully grasped the nuances of lawyers. His mind would read between the lines and not be swayed by superfluous arguments of advocates who had taken high fees from clients. In the last fifteen years, Judge Sushil Kumar had created a reputation of an honest and efficient judge.

The court room of Judge Sushil Kumar was almost full. Most of the chairs were occupied by advocates and their assistants. In a barricaded portion of the courtroom sat several undertrials. Most of them were not interested in court proceedings. In a corner sat Manoj, although his eyes were apparently fixed towards the judge, he seemed absent minded. His countenance portrayed his remorse. It was at 11.18 am that the court clerk, in a voice not fully a shout but slightly above normal decibel, announced Case number 840 of 2022, St Andrews College, State vs Manoj Singh. Hearing his name, Manoj became attentive, his gaze shifted to the two advocates who had picked their files and moved forward towards the podium in front of Judge Sushil Kumar to argue. Manoj recognised his lawyer. On several occasions Aftab Ahmad had met him in jail to take notes of the events that preceded and followed the murder of Father Joseph, the Principal of St Andrews College, for which Manoj has been charged with murder. Manoj didn't recognise the other advocate, he thought that this advocate was perhaps representing the St Andrews College.

The counsel for the petitioner started to argue. In a practiced measured tone, he started his argument by extolling the virtues of Father Joseph who was loved by one and all. He told the court that Father Joseph was an extremely humble person who had devoted his life to the service of mankind in the name of Jesus. Father Joseph had no enemies. The counsel for the petitioner took a long pause, this was not a pause for recalling notes but he wanted this information to sink in the mind of the judge before he proceeded further.

The counsel for St Andrews College continued, he started narrating the events of that fateful Thursday which was the tenth of February 2022. He told the court that some students had not submitted their fee for the last couple of months despite numerous reminders. It was after several reminders that the Principal of St Andrews College had sent a message to all parents to personally report in his office on February tenth. At this point the counsel pointed a finger towards Manoj in the undertrial box. Everybody turned towards the man sitting on a stool in the trial box. Judge Sushil Kumar also looked at him. Manoj felt a bout of nausea when he realised that everyone was looking at him. The counsel continued his argument. He told the court that Manoj's son had not deposited his fee for the last three months and this was told to Manoj by Father in a very polite way. Manoj had protested in a defiant way and asked for more time to deposit the fee. Father Andrews had told Manoj that his son will not be allowed to appear for examination if the fee was not deposited till this evening.

The Counsel again took a long pause, he glanced at the other lawyer who was representing Manoj, he veered his gaze towards Manoj in the undertrial box. The Counsel was satisfied that his argument was hitting the bull's eye. He continued his argument telling the court that Manoj had behaved badly and had threatened Father Joseph of dire consequences if his son was not allowed to appear in his final examination. At this point Judge Sushil Kumar, without any reason, looked towards Manoj in the undertrial box. His mind was trying to find out why this innocent looking man would behave rudely with a polite Principal. While his eyes searched for those invisible cues which Judge Sushil Kumar's mind had become so accustomed to recognise, his eighty-six billion neurons found another reason to fire. A remote corner of his mind was prompting his brain that this man who was sitting on the stool in the undertrial box was known to him. Judge Sushil Kumar again looked towards the presenting Counsel who was beginning a new narrative.

The Counsel addressing the Judge continued that on February 10, 2022 when Manoj was furiously arguing with Father Joseph, he had become infuriated. The counsel told the court that on the fateful day when Manoj was abusing father Joseph, Father stood from his chair and wanted to go out of the room. It was at this point that Manoj had picked up the heavy glass paper weight from the table and hit Father Joseph on his head. After being hit on the back of the skull by the trajectile thrown by Manoj, Father had collapsed. The Counsel again took a break. He looked towards Manoj and in a tone which was an octave higher to his previous decibel, pointing his index finger, said that My Lord this man is a murderer. He murdered Father Joseph in cold blood. This is a murder of not only a man but of the society. The Father was revered not only because of his faith but because of his selfless service to the society.

There was pin drop silence in the courtroom. Judge Sushil Kumar again looked towards Manoj. Manoj looked forlorn. Although his eyes were open but he was not looking towards anyone. For a moment his eyes met Judge Sushil Kumar's sight. Manoj saw the heavy eyebrows above those penetrating eyes. A thought crossed his mind but he could not latch upon the reason why his brain had become active. Manoj's thought returned to the proceedings of the court. He knew that the petitioner's counsel had by and large narrated the exact sequence of events. It was a different matter that the counsel had played with certain facts to make his case strong. Manoj recollected that in February 2022, he was in great debt, he had lost his job due to COVID. It was only one month back in January that his wife had died due to cancer. On the day when Father had called him in his office, he had pleaded with Father Joseph with tears in his eyes to give him one more month for depositing the fee of his son. He had told Father that after the death of his wife, his son was the only one left in his family. Manoj also recollected that he had literally begged Father to allow his son to take the examination, he didn't want his son to be a fifth-class dropout due to economic reasons. Manoj's thought also relived the traumatic memory how he had wept and pleaded with Father telling him that almost thirty years back he had to leave the same school in fifth standard when his father had died, in fact, murdered, and how subsequently he left school due to the family's inability to pay the fee.

Manoj's eyes focused on the proceedings. His counsel Aftab Ahmad was organising his file and was about to commence his argument. Manoj's mind again drifted to his thoughts. He remembered that in a show of gesture of humility, he had kneeled down and grasped the feet of Father Joseph pleading that his son be given one month more time to deposit fee. At that very moment the school bell had rung and Father had started to rise from his chair. Manoj could recollect the face of the Father while he was pleading with tears in his eyes. There was no kindness in Father's eyes. Suddenly he saw that Father was walking out of his office. Manoj recollected the moment when in a fit of rage, he had picked the paper weight from the table and threw it towards Father Joseph. The paper weight hit Father Joseph just above the neck and he collapsed. Manoj remembered that he too was dazed after the incident. He didn't try to flee and surrendered without any resistance.

Aftab Ahmad started his argument by pointing a finger at Manoj who was now too dazed after hearing the first argument. At Aftab Ahmad's insistence when Judge Sushil Kumar looked at Manoj, Aftab Ahmad in a pleading voice asked the Judge whether the man sitting inside the prisoner enclosure looks like a criminal who would go to a school with the intent of murder. Aftab was deliberately playing on the mind of Judge who had a reputation of forming opinion based on his own perception. Aftab continued his argument. He told the judge that his client is a man of modest means and he was very hard pressed since he lost his job during COVID. Aftab argued that Manoj had lost his wife just one month before this unfortunate incident had happened on February 10, 2022.

The argument of Aftab was going in the right direction. From the faces of other lawyers in the courtroom it was apparent that Aftab had weaved a solid alibi for the crime for which Manoj was being tried. Aftab continued that Manoj had suffered many hardships since childhood. While Manoj was a student of class V in the same school, the St Andrews College, some thirty years back, his father was murdered by land mafia syndicate. Despite the fact that Manoj was one of the brightest students in class he had to leave studies since the family had no means to pay college fee. Manoj had completed basic level education from vernacular school and then got a private job. He had lost this private job during COVID.

Judge Sushil Kumar was listening intently to the argument. He was amazed that even after an hour of argument the Counsel representing

Manoj had not countered the charge that Manoj had actually murdered Father Joseph. However, despite the silent admission of the crime, Judge Sushil Kumar felt that Manoj's crime was probably not premeditated and that it was a result of circumstances which went back to thirty years. As Aftab continued to argue, he came to the events of February ten narrating Manoj's version of how he had pleaded with Father Joseph, the clock struck signaling the end of days schedule. The judge adjourned the case for the next day.

On way to home Judge Sushil Kumar kept on thinking about the case where a man was charged with a crime of murder. However, for him the intriguing part was that the man under trial looked familiar. He recollected how his brain had flagged the moment when he first saw the man in the trial box. Judge Sushil Kumar's mind started to fill the gaps in the memory of his mind.

By the time he reached his home, Judge Sushil Kumar had created a hypothesis in his mind. He wanted to cross check it before he proceeded further. Once inside his house, he went to the attic and fished out the large trunk where he had stored all the papers, diaries, documents and other items after his father's death. Once settled in his room, he started leafing through the old papers, diaries and registers. He found the diary where his father had chronicled his business deals and other important facts during the period between January to December 1978. He patiently went through all the details. There was a detailed mention of some conversation with his business partners and some difference of opinion with someone named Santosh Singh. At a later stage a mention was made which said that 'problem eliminated'. The Judge's mind took note of this veiled mention by his father. His mind started filling the gaps. The hypothesis in his mind looked true.

Judge Sushil Kumar went back in the attic and fished out his own trunk in which he had stored all his school records. Surfing documents in this lot was easier, he knew what he was searching. Within minutes he had chanced upon the old manila envelope which contained all his old photographs from school days when the only means to have a photograph was through a hard copy. As he glanced through the bundle, it was within five minutes that he had the group photograph of Class V A of St Andrews School. His eyes searched for a kid named Manoj Singh. Judge Sushil Kumar's mind took less than a quarter of a second to connect the lanky boy standing in the second row to the undertrial Manoj who was sitting helplessly on a stool in the convict chamber of Court number three this morning. Judge Sushil Kumar knew he had solved the mystery which his mind had detected when he first saw Manoj Singh, the undertrial.

That night when Judge Sushil Kumar went to bed having skipped dinner on the pretext that he was not feeling well, he felt heavy in the chest. By this time his mind had filled all the pieces of the puzzle in the correct format. The forty five year old Manoj Singh, accused of cold blooded murder of Father Joseph, was his classmate some thirty years back in St Andrews. Judge Sushil Kumar recollected that Manoj Singh was very bright and always stood first or second in class. Manoj was also a close friend at that time and suddenly he had stopped coming to class. Judge Sushil Kumar now recollected that Manoj also did not appear in the final examination. Time passed and everyone had forgotten Manoj Singh.

Judge Sushil Kumar's memory flashback reached the point where he realised that Manoj's absence from the school was linked to the demise of his father and the inability of the family to pay the school fee. The realisation by Judge Sushil Kumar that his own father had orchestrated the murder of Manoj's father made him sick. A feeling of disdain emerged from his heart and he silently cursed his father for a crime which cannot be justified. His judicial mind came to the conclusion that the murder for which Manoj was being tried today was in fact committed some thirty years back by his father. The deeper Judge Sushil Kumar taxed his brain, more emotions came pouring in. He started to feel the pain of a young child barely in his teens losing his father to an untimely sudden death. He perceived the trauma that a young Manoj Singh must have felt when at an early age he had to work to earn a living. Sushil Kumar felt the intense distress of a helpless father when the man had begged the Principal of St Andrews school to grant one more month to his son for depositing fee. Judge Sushil Kumar felt a strange sense of melancholy. He continued to ask himself the question as to how he would have behaved if he was wearing Manoj's shoes? On several occasions that night Judge Sushil Kumar wanted to blurt out the answer to this question but he was afraid to acknowledge the naked reality of life. Judge Sushil Kumar felt weak. He lay in bed but sleep eluded him the whole night.

Manoj's case again came up before Judge Sushil Kumar the next day. Arguments started. It was Aftab Ahmad who started with his unfinished argument. Aftab Ahmad focused on the false premise that Father Joseph was killed by an innocuous strike by a small paper weight. He elaborated his argument by opening several other possibilities. Aftab Ahmad placed before the Judge medical records of Father Joseph which showed that Father was a heart patient and thus, he could have suffered a fatal cardiac arrest just at the time when he stood from his chair even before Manoj threw the paper weight. Aftab Ahmad continued to argue for a good ninety minutes giving several possible examples which could have been the reason of Father Joseph's death. While both the Counsels were arguing their cases, Judge Sushil Kumar's mind was still playing back the information which he had gathered from his father's diary last evening. In between he glanced towards Manoj who looked paler than yesterday. Every time he saw this forty-five-year-old man, his brain recollected the image of a lanky eleven-year-old boy happily playing cricket in the St Andrews School field.

The arguments in Manoj's case closed at lunch. The judge announced a new date when the two sides would present witnesses for their testimony. New cases flooded Court Number three. However, in between the varied cases listed before Judge Sushil Kumar, he found it hard to erase the lingering thought of Manoj. At frequent intervals his mind reminded him that had Manoj not lost his father in early childhood he too would have been in a good position, much like him. If that had been the case, Manoj would not be pleading for school fee and he would not have committed the murder for which he was facing this trial.

Manoj's case lingered in Court for three more months. The arguments had closed. The Counsel representing St Andrews College had proved without doubt that Father Joseph was killed by the hit on his skull by the paper weight thrown at him by Manoj. The Counsel had pleaded for death sentence. Aftab Ahmad, Manoj's advocate, had harped on the fact that Manoj had no intention to kill or harm the Principal. Aftab Ahmad had also pleaded that the Judge may like to consider the circumstances which preceded the events of February 10, 2022 and be lenient on Manoj.

Since the murder of Father Joseph had been the talk of the town for a long-time last year, a horde of media had assembled to cover the delivery of judgement on December 20, 2023 at the Sessions Court. Aftab Ahmad had requested the Court to allow Anuj, the eleven-year-old son of Manoj, to come to the Court on the judgement day. The Court had granted permission.

The Sessions Court premises exuded the same busy atmosphere on December 20, 2023. As usual the lawyers walked in quick strides. The tea sellers had a motley crowd on their stalls. A few policemen, oblivious of the judgements inside courtrooms, found stools and chairs to sit in areas where they could get sunlight. The arrival of the blue armored police van also looked a usual sight. This happened every day. Today when the prisoners came out escorted by lazy looking police guards, Manoj was also in that group. In the last three months he had lost some weight. He looked lost and silently followed the policeman who escorted him to Court number three.

The Court number three was jam packed. Lawyers in hushed tones were discussing what Judge Sushil Kumar was going to decide. In the back bench of the court, a young eleven-year-old boy was sitting. Anuj had by now understood what today's judgement meant for him. After his mother had died last year, he had no other person to look up to except his father. He knew today's judgment may change everything.

It was just before fifteen past ten that a frail looking Manoj was escorted inside the enclosure of undertrials. Anuj eyes looked intently towards his father, he wanted to make eye contact with his father but the din inside the courtroom prevented any possible communication. A few minutes later the man in white uniform announced that everyone must stand, the Judge was about to enter the Courtroom.

Proceedings started with the clerk announcing Case number 840 of 2022. Although there was no scope for any arguments at this stage but both the Counsels, one representing St Andrews College and other representing Manoj stood up from their chairs and took their positions before the Judge.

Judge Sushil Kumar looked stoic. He opened the file kept on his table. He leafed a few pages and then addressed Counsel for Manoj asking him whether his request for allowing Manoj's son to witness Court proceedings has been granted. Aftab Ahmad nodded his head in the affirmative muttering 'My Lord'. The Judge asked the Counsel to bring Manoj's son before the court. Anuj was escorted to the front. Judge Sushil Kumar saw Anuj. No one could see but the Judge's eyes were wet. Judge Sushil Kumar's memory took him back thirty years, in that fleeting moment his mind superimposed the image of an eleven-year-old Manoj. The Judge again felt a lump in his throat. Anuj stood there under the glare of peering eyes. His gaze met the sight of Manoj. The silent conversation between a convicted father and a teenage helpless son made everyone wondering about the vagaries of destiny.

Judge Sushil Kumar instructed that Anuj be escorted back to his place in the back row. Without any preamble he started delivering the judgement. The first part of the judgement dealt with the details of events of February 2022. Dwelling more on legal nuances which took another ten minutes, Judge Sushil Kumar started delivering the operative part. He started '***it is proved beyond doubt that the death of Father Joseph was caused by a hit on his head by the heavy paper weight thrown towards him by Manoj Singh. The Court has gone into the history of Manoj Singh and observes that Manoj Singh has no criminal history associated with his records. The prosecution failed to establish that when Manoj Singh came to the office of the***

Principal on February 10, 2022, he carried the intent to harm the Principal. To the court it is obvious that Manoj Singh wanted to seek more time for depositing the fee of his son. The Court relying on records supplied by the College is convinced that Manoj Singh's son Anuj was a very bright student in Class V and that after that fateful day he has been forced to leave school. In view of the facts and circumstances cited above, the Court finds Manoj Singh guilty of culpable homicide under Section 304 of the IPC. He will undergo Life Imprisonment'.

The Courtroom was in silence. It is not often that a convict is given life imprisonment. Judge Sushil Kumar continued ***'this Court directs the administration of St Andrews College to give admission to the son of convict Manoj Singh without any preconditions. A sealed letter will be delivered to the Principal of St Andrews College detailing how the fee will be charged from Anuj Singh. A sealed letter will also be delivered to the District Magistrate detailing how other expenses and higher education of Anuj Singh will be covered'.***

Two days later the Management Council of St Andrews College convened an emergency meeting wherein the official letter received from Judge Sushil Kumar was opened. The document was a note with a signature of a notary bearing the affidavit of Sushil Kumar. The affidavit said that till the time Anuj Singh is a student of St Andrews College the fee will be paid directly to the college by Mr Sushil Kumar. No mention of this has to be made to Anuj Singh.

A couple of kilometers away, a similar exercise was underway in the office of the District Magistrate. A similar affidavit affirmed that all expenses of Anuj Singh from today and till he completes his higher education will be covered from a bank account mentioned below. This arrangement may be treated as a judicial order and also be considered strictly confidential.

The Last Laugh

The snakes had not been fed for the last two days. Tonight, Suresh had put the rat catcher at three different places, he expected to catch three rats which will be enough for his snakes for the next few days. The reflecting glass of the lantern perched on the far wall was coated with thick soot. The faint light emitted from the kerosene burning wick provided just enough light for Suresh to see the contours of his ramshackle cottage. He had lived in this cottage for the last forty years. Lying on his misnomer bed made of old straw, he could easily hear the rumblings of the flowing water in Yamuna River. The river was just a stone's throw from his cottage.

Tonight, Suresh found it hard to sleep. The events of the day were difficult to forget. It was around noon that he had a few visitors who had used abusive language against him and threatened that if he did not vacate this cottage within the next three days, it will be treated as a disobedience to 'bhai' and the repercussions may be difficult. Suresh knew for sure that the tone of the threat was grave. Since the last several months 'bhai's' men had purchased or usurped all the land around his cottage. It was in the air that 'bhai' wanted to build a riverside resort on the banks of the scenic Yamuna riverfront. For several months Suresh had withstood his ground and had even refused money from 'bhai's' henchmen. As Suresh lay wide awake on that night waiting to hear the clicking sound of the mouse trap, he glanced at his wife and son lying on makeshift straw beds deep in sleep.

While it was almost pitch dark in Suresh's cottage, just a kilometer away, the night had just unfolded in 'bhai's' mansion. The entrance of the sprawling mansion was dotted with top end cars and SUVs. Most vehicles sported the insignia of different political parties. Inside the mansion, the party was in full swing. On the center table 'bhai' was in deep conversation with some of his close confidantes. There were different groups of people all engrossed in loud banter which covered an assortment of topics ranging from politics to Indian cricket team. The importance of each person was advertised by the number of security personnel standing beside him.

Suresh considered this a lucky omen that he could capture three rats soon in each of his rat catcher devices. Silently he went to the far end of his cottage and removed the flimsy cloth which till now was shielding the bamboo-stick circular flat cages wherein his snakes were housed. Opening each cage a few inches, he put one rat each in all the three cages. He made a mental note that within a few days he was required to extract the venom. For the last twenty years Suresh had made a living by selling snake venom to agents who scouted for this deadly poison. Some of the agents had fleetingly told him that snake venom found use in medicines for treatment of paralysis and muscle pain. Suresh found this explanation weird but fancied no reason to disbelief till the time he got paid in cash.

The party in 'bhai's' mansion was in its last leg. The crowd had thinned. There were only a couple of guests who had 'bhai's' ears. It was in between this secret conversation that 'bhai' asked someone to look for Prabhas, his son. Prabhas had a different coterie, his group had selected a far end of the lawn slightly removed from his father's line of sight. On a cue from a silent messenger, Prabhas went to 'bhai's' table. The conversation revolved around the resistance of the snake charmer to move out of the cottage. 'Bhai' was livid at the incompetence of his henchmen. In a veiled and encouraging language, 'bhai' asked Prabhas to get the job done. This was perhaps, as 'bhai' thought, the first real assignment for Prabhas.

It had drizzled the whole day. Already depressed from the events of a couple of days back, Suresh had remained in his cottage doing nothing. He was so attached to his cottage that he didn't want to leave it. Pappu, his son, gave him company. It was in the afternoon that Suresh opened his snakes. His watchful eyes silently allowed Pappu to fiddle with the reptiles. As evening drifted into darkness, his wife offered him fish curry and rice. The family partook the meal with scant conversation. Night descended early while it rained outside. The lantern again started emitting its faint glow.

Suresh lost count of time while he had remained awake thinking about 'bhai's' threat. As his thoughts meandered to various options, he dozed off. The knock on the door was menacingly ugly. As Suresh struggled to find his senses from deep slumber, the old wooden door of the cottage fell down. In the dim light of the soot coated lantern, Suresh caught sight of the silhouette of three men. He could recognise only Prabhas among the three intruders. In the commotion, Suresh opened his mouth to yell but the bullet pierced his neck before his lungs could push the air through his larynx. Suresh fell down on Pappu who was lying just beside him. The second bullet found its target on the chest of Suresh's wife. An eerie silence followed the two gunshots. Just fifty meters away the serene Yamuna continued its last journey in the joyous anticipation of meeting Ganges. The three men left the cottage without a word. Pappu already soaked with his father's blood was too terrified to wriggle out from the weight of the dead body lying above him.

As morning ended the darkness of the night, curious onlookers flocked the cottage. Someone had put a few pieces of cloth on the bodies of Suresh and his wife. An onlooker offered biscuit and tea to Pappu who was still dazed to weep or talk. While a motley crowd made arrangements for the last rites, nobody found courage to delve into the cause of death. It was just after sunset that a JCB trudged on the marshy land towards the cottage where Suresh used to live.

A camouflaged smile greeted Prabhas when he joined his father during breakfast. 'Bhai' had already been informed about the clinical precision how Prabhas had liquidated the snake charmer and his wife last night. 'Bhai' beckoned his son to sit next to him on the breakfast table. In the next ten minutes he detailed to his son how he wanted to develop the riverfront into an open amphitheater with a rooftop restaurant. As he finished his tea, he put a hand on Prabhas's shoulder and said 'well done'. While the don and the heir apparent were making plans for the vast open land where the lone remaining cottage of Suresh had been razed last evening, Pappu was still too dazed from the events which had unfolded. Tonight, as he found refuge in the old rag picker's house, his sleep was broken several times with the dream in which he saw the cold face of a young man pointing a revolver at his father. The face of that young man had been etched in his mind.

As time passed, 'bhai' gave more and more of his responsibilities to Prabhas. In Prabhas, 'bhai' had the confidence of full dedication and utmost secrecy. On his part, Prabhas picked the nuances of the underworld very fast. A few years had passed and Prabhas had acquired the status of a ruthless underworld don. 'Bhai' had taken a back seat and Prabhas controlled the sprawling empire of crime in his indomitable style. His fear percolated the society and administration alike. After 'bhai's' sudden mysterious death, which as rumours were whispered implicating his son's desire for an early takeover, Prabhas established himself as the sole and undisputed leader of the vast crime syndicate.

While it had taken fifteen years for Prabhas to take the pole position in the crime world of the city, Pappu had witnessed many upheavals in his life. The rag picker who had initially given him refuge after the death of his father and mother, sold him to a begging cartel. To make him suitable for begging, Pappu's leg was ruthlessly broken and then plastered in a way so as to create a permanent disability. In less than six months, Pappu, with a crooked leg, became an ideal beggar who earned not for himself but for his masters who lived-in air-conditioned houses and commuted in swanky cars. As Pappu became an adult he detested his condition. On the streets, while he begged, he saw many strange things. At times he knew more than the local police intelligence unit. After a few years Pappu broke free from the hold of the begging gang and begged for himself soliciting money from the affluent community of the neighbourhood. Since nobody knew about his real name, he would target some houses on

Tuesdays and some on Thursdays, playing on the human adherence for religious beliefs. His style earned him constant alms. On the streets Pappu recognised Prabhas when his entourage would pass through the street. Pappu would invariably get that dreaded dream when he saw Prabhas.

Although Prabhas was now the king of the underworld, he still preferred to handle sensitive killings himself. Sometimes even his closest confidantes and gang members were unaware when Prabhas would undertake a solo adventure. This was Prabhas's style of functioning and by this modus operandi he would invariably leave no trace behind or any accomplice who may later spill the secret.

As time passed, Prabhas wanted to expand his clout which was already high in the world of crime. He realised that to go beyond this point he had to foray into politics. The elections for the State Assembly were a few months away and Prabhas decided to transfer his criminal influence to electoral politics. Although he had friends in all political parties but he chose the ruling party and joined it in the presence of a few state level leaders with a fanfare that overnight became the talk of the town. Post his political entry, Prabhas started exploring options how to get the party ticket for the elections. The sitting MLA was an established leader with almost two decades of experience as a lawmaker and enjoyed decent support from the central leadership of the ruling party. Prabhas realised that his chances of replacing the sitting MLA could only be accomplished if somehow, he could liquidate the person. The ruthless criminal mind of Prabhas started conjuring plots.

On two consecutive nights Prabhas went on a reconnaissance mission to the residence of the MLA which was just a kilometer from his own residence. Prabhas noted that the MLA moved around in the company of a private security personnel and had an escort police vehicle. On the second night he noted that the four police constables were always complacent. Among the four police constables, only one was armed.

It was a dark night when at around ten in the night Prabhas

silently left his mansion from the rear door. None of his accomplices knew about this secret endeavour. For several years now Prabhas had always presented himself in public in all white attire but for this mission he wore khaki cargo trousers and a military worn out T shirt. He carried two revolvers, a Taurus 327 and a 2.7mm Kolibri. Today he took a different route to the residence of the MLA. The gates were closed but from his previous recce he knew that invariably the MLA returned at around eleven in the night.

Prabhas hid behind a bend and waited. The siren of the police escort at ten past eleven alerted him. The MLA alighted from his vehicle accompanied by his personal security guard. The police van remained closed. The adrenal gland pumped a dose of epinephrine in Prabhas's blood. Clutching his Taurus 327 revolver he approached the MLA from a side lane. Prabhas moved silently putting a poaching leopard to shame. He came within ten meters of his target. From a far corner of his sight the security guard caught the movement, he turned to face the intruder but did not live to see his face. The bullet caught his side temple even before his eighty-six billion neurons could decipher what was going on. The second bullet hit the MLA on the chest. A second later a fountain of blood gushed out. The sound of gunshots jolted the half sleeping constables and they struggled to come out of their vehicle. Prabhas was already on his way back taking long strides but showing no signs of panic.

Years of escort duty had made the four police constables lose focus on the job. The sight of two dead bodies including one who they were supposed to guard made them spring to action. As they were scrambling from their vehicle, one of them had seen a silhouette take the lane leading to the main road. The four police men started running following the shadow of the man who was now beyond sight. At the bend, as they ran full steam, they caught sight of a moving shadow almost fifty meters ahead walking briskly.

Walking at a speed just shy of a trot, a sixth sense prompted Prabhas that he was being followed. Without slowing his pace, he glanced behind and saw four policemen running towards him.

Prabhas had to go straight but his instincts told him that he had no time. Suddenly he turned right and took the narrow lane. His intuition prompted him to look for a hiding place. Prabhas spotted a makeshift hut in a corner. He rushed inside. Pappu was already in his worn-out bed of old straw stuffed mattress. Today he was late to sleep since he had to feed his snakes and had to catch the rats. He sprang to a sitting position as someone barged into his small tent. The man seemed frightened. His eyes were searching for a place to hide. It took less than a few seconds for Pappu to recognise that the man, looking highly vulnerable to an invisible threat, was Prabhas. Pappu's mind suddenly recalled the moment when as a five-year-old he had seen the same face pump bullets in his father and mother's body.

In that split second Pappu debated a plethora of options, he realised that his heart and mind did not concur. He decided to follow his mind. Pappu gestured to the intruder to come to his bed and lie down. Once the intruder was in supine position, Pappu put all his clothes on top of the person making a mound of soiled clothes. Finally, he covered everything with an old bedsheet. Pappu took his place lying down where he was sleeping.

The policemen lost sight of the fleeing man while they ran in pursuit. As they came to the bend where the road gave way to a narrow path, they felt unsure which way to follow. On cue, two policemen went inside the lane and two stayed on the road running ahead. The two policemen who had taken the narrow lane had no idea where this lane went. They found a lone hut at a broader area of the kerb. One of the policemen with the gun, pushed the old cloth hanging at the entrance and entered the hut. Pappu expected this. Purposefully he made an effort to get up rubbing his eyes as if waking from deep slumber. The panting policeman asked whether he had seen someone pass by. Pappu nodded his head in negative. The policeman convinced of the truthfulness of the beggar left the hut.

It had been decades since Prabhas could recollect when he had last visited a temple, however today, lying motionless under a pile of stinking clothes he thanked all the Gods he knew. After twenty minutes he pushed his camouflage aside and got up. He saw Pappu, a man with a characteristic face and a broken leg. Prabhas wanted to give this man something but had nothing except his two revolvers. Leaving the hut, he mumbled something which Pappu did not understand. As Prabhas walked out of the hut, Pappu's face sported a crooked smile.

The murder of the MLA and his security guard became a hot news. Prabhas was among the first political leader to visit the MLA's house and offer his condolences. The Police Commissioner was under immense pressure to solve the crime. He immediately suspended the four policemen who were on escort duty. It was within forty-eight hours that the police announced at a hurriedly convened press conference that they have arrested four persons and the gang has confessed to the crime. Public memory is ephemeral and it took only a couple of days before the murder of the MLA was lost in the cacophony of other crime stories.

The election was announced and Prabhas was the front runner to get the ticket of the ruling party for fighting the election. He got the ticket. Such was his terror that ardent supporters of other political parties displayed Prabhas's party flag on top of their houses. Roadside banners proclaimed that Prabhas and his family have always worked for the underprivileged class of the society. Petty political leaders conducted mass campaigns singing paeans of the philanthropy of Prabhas. Election came and went. Prabhas won the election with a record margin of votes.

With government machinery at his disposal, Prabhas found his empire flourishing without any hiccups. He started extending his influence on other MLAs not only of his party but from other political parties too. Within a couple of years, he was able to engineer a split in the main opposition party, much to the appreciation of his party high command. Prabhas emerged as the new blue-eyed boy of the political scene.

Five years passed by in a jiffy. Next elections were round the corner. Prabhas was an automatic choice for the party ticket to fight the election. This time he was also consulted by the high command before ticket distribution in other neighbouring constituencies. In the elections, Prabhas again won by a high margin of votes. For his influence within the party Prabhas was given a Cabinet rank with the Medical Department under his charge.

The new found Cabinet rank meant more power. Prabhas started to enjoy his influence not only in the city but also in the whole state. Frequently Prabhas found coverage in print and digital media. At places around the city, big billboards displayed his smiling photographs with different slogans. The gullible voters found no reason to doubt the integrity of the Honourable Minister. The Minister became a demi God!

Pappu's life had not changed. As per his schedule he begged collecting alms on Tuesdays and Thursday and also sold venom to agents from his two snakes which he kept in his hut. At times when he saw a smiling Prabhas face on a billboard, his mind would wander to that fateful day when he first looked at this face with horror while his father was shot dead. His other memory took him to that fateful night when this smiling face was terron stricken and had found refuge in his hut. At times Pappu felt remorse of having not alerted the policeman on that night.

Greed is something which has no boundaries. Within a couple of years of becoming a cabinet minister, Prabhas started dreaming of becoming the Chief Minister. Prabhas realised that this was a tall order. There was no way the current Chief Minister could be replaced. Prabhas started thinking in a different direction. He stumbled upon a plan.

The second anniversary of the Government was approaching and Prabhas floated a proposal in the cabinet to organise a grand felicitation function for the Chief Minister. As part of the proposal, a big function would be organised in the constituency of Prabhas which will be attended by the Chief Minister. Every politician loves adulation and the Chief Minister was no different. The proposal was approved.

The Intelligence unit of the Police received a call which made several people concerned. A caller from an unknown number methodically mentioned that an assassination attempt would be made against the Chief Minister in the felicitation function. Within minutes the State Intelligence Bureau was searching for the origin of the call. The buck stopped at a roadside, almost defunct, public call office. It was difficult to find the person who had made the call. In less than an hour the Chief Minister was informed about the threat.

The date of the function was fast approaching. The administration was on its toes, the venue was being constantly monitored by plain clothes intelligence personnel. The police had prepared a full SOP to ensure security.

Prabhas too felt the pressure of Chief Minister's function. He too had a lot of unfinished agenda, albeit in a different direction. Just a week remained for the function. Following his own devised algorithm, Prabhas's mind never required any written SOPs. He asked his office to book his air tickets for Mumbai. Tonight, he made a mental note to call his film producer friend for a personal favour. Last night he had already called an accomplice in Mumbai to arrange for an AK-47 rifle for a day.

While in his hotel room in Mumbai, Prabhas had many visitors. Mostly it was the political cadre which wanted to interact with the rising star of the ruling political party. In the night Prabhas moved to a secret destination which was only accessible to a few select old friends. His film producer friend informed him that as per Prabhas's request he had booked the Sonic Octaves Sound Recording Studio in Malad West. At around midnight through a discreet messenger Prabhas received a sealed bag containing the AK-47 rifle with a fully loaded seventy-five round magazine.

The Sonic Octaves Sound Recording Studio was a professional recording studio which catered to all kinds of recording jobs. The staff had become so used to their work that they seldom paid any heed to the final outcome of their work. Professionally the supervisor of the recording unit listened to what his client wanted this Friday morning and accomplished the recording. It was within three hours that Prabhas took a taxi from Malad West to his hotel. The sixty-four GB pendrive was the only addition which he had taken from the recording studio. After returning the AK-47 to the underworld accomplice, Prabhas took the return flight in the afternoon.

Just three days remained for the felicitation function of the Chief Minister. The huge fire proof tent was already in its place. At any given time, hundreds of policemen guarded the venue. The State Intelligence Department was already monitoring the phone of a large number of known criminals and opposition politicians in the hope of getting advance intelligence on any possible assassination attempt. The metal detectors had been installed and every person was being frisked. The local MLA who was also the cabinet minister for Medical Department was constantly monitoring all the preparations. He had issued strict instructions for a fool proof security.

Prabhas made some important transfers in his department just a couple of days before the felicitation function. The doctors in the emergency wing of the district hospital were transferred. Officially it was notified that this was being done to bring the best doctors in the district hospital before the important function.

The mega tent was finally ready. The stage where the Chief Minister was to sit had been thoroughly sanitised by several layers of security. The terraces of the high-rise buildings around the tent ground had both hidden and obvious sharp shooters who continuously scanned the horizon and the road for any suspicious activity. The sound system inside the tent had been checked including the speaker boxes for any hidden explosive devices. The Police Commissioner had set up a camp office inside the tent to oversee the security detail.

While everything was ready, the sound system incharge had suddenly reported ill. There was a panic like condition in the organising committee and as per instructions, this message was faithfully transmitted to Prabhas for further instructions. A calm and composed Prabhas informed the Police Commissioner that he is sending a person who shall control the sound system. Within ten minutes a new sound system operator was at his work. He checked all the systems and found that the system was working fine.

Prabhas noted that all his preparations were complete. The doctors had been instructed at the District Hospital and in the ambulance, the sound operator was in full command and the two injections of ketamine were already kept in the pockets of his Nehru Jacket. Just thirty minutes remained for the event. The Chief Minister's helicopter had already landed in the adjacent ground. Prabhas had gone to welcome him.

The stage was elegantly decorated. Only two persons were on the dais. A horde of gun totting security took their position behind the Chief Minister. The two flower bouquet meant to be presented to the Chief Minister and Prabhas had been sanitized by two separate security teams. The function started with the lighting of the traditional lamp.

The sound operator took out the pen drive from his pocket and inserted it in the sound system. He looked at his watch. A couple of minutes were left when he had to start the pen drive. As the clock struck sixty seconds, the sound operator pressed the 'play' button. It was at this moment that the Chief Minister was getting up from his Chair to address the crowd. In respect of the Chair, the cabinet minister had also risen from the chair.

The crowd heard the rapid firing of chilling automatic gunfire, everyone was stunned. Nobody knew from where the AK-47 was being fired. The security was taken by surprise. Some took evasive action and some scrambled to hold their weapons. On the stage there was a state of melee. The Chief Minister involuntarily ducked to shield himself from the unknown line of fire. His cabinet colleague hugged the Chief Minister in a show of protection. Both the men fell down on the stage. It was in that frenzy, while the tent reverberated with intermittent gun fire, that Prabhas silently pushed the needle of his ketamine loaded syringe through the 'kurta' of the Chief Minister. The CM already under the weight of Prabhas felt a twitch but with his heart beating like a sparrow from fresh adrenaline, he remained still.

There was utter commotion in the tent, people ran for shelter. The security personnel felt clueless to pin point the source of the gunfire. The ambulance team arrived within a minute. The doctor on duty tried to resuscitate the CM but he was unconscious. Prabhas had gained composure and fervently yelled to take the CM to the hospital. It was within a couple of minutes that an unconscious CM was on his way to the district hospital with an entourage which included Prabhas's official car.

The CM was wheeled on a stretcher inside the emergency ward of the hospital. The two doctors on duty felt the pulse, it was palpable. Professionally the other doctor inserted a cannula and connected the saline drip. Silently he took out a syringe from the refrigerator which had two hundred units of insulin and pushed the contents in the saline bottle.

Within minutes, a crowd had swelled outside the hospital. The police were having a tough time controlling the media persons. Prabhas stood at the gate of the ward looking immensely worried. It was after thirty minutes that one of the doctors emerged from the ward and briefed the media persons. In measured terms he said that the CM had suffered a cardiac arrest and that he was in a critical condition.

The insulin started working. Still comatose from ketamine, the CM had no idea that his blood glucose was steadily reaching the critical point. A few drops of perspiration trickled on his forehead. His pulse became weak and slow. The high dose of insulin was still at work. The CM's brain stopped working; it took another thirty minutes for the heart to stop.

Within minutes all the TV channels began breaking the news of CM's death. There were many angles to the story. From gunshot injury to cardiac arrest, the verdict was split. The story of gunfire in the CM's event was also being debated. Most of the TV channels ascribed this assassination as a security lapse. One reporter who was present on the scene did report that despite the sound of the gunfire, no shots were fired. The story of CM's assassination was so dominant that the actual events at the function were lost in the ensuing debates.

In Delhi the Central Leadership also took stock of the death of a sitting CM. Politics is all about eulogising the present, the past has no relevance. All the talk in the Central Leadership focused on finding the new CM. Although there was a debate but most members agreed that the best candidate would be the present Cabinet Minister Prabhas Shukla.

Even before the cremation of the former CM, a silent celebration was underway in Prabhas's mansion. News had percolated that the Central Leadership had decided upon his name as the new CM.

The official news on the selection of the new CM was given to the Governor the next day. Prabhas was also duly communicated the date and time of swearing in. Prabhas felt a sense of satisfaction, not for the fact that he was going to the CM but for the reason that he had executed a perfect plan. His brain started secreting dopamine.

The road was lined with an unending long queue of cars. All sported the insignia of the ruling party. The walls were plastered with the beaming face of Prabhas Shukla. News had come that the new CM would soon be going to Raj Bhawan to take the oath.

While it had taken just under twenty years for Prabhas to become the CM, the intervening years had been a long and painful journey for Pappu. Life had been very cruel to him. His broken leg was always in pain. Every night when he slept on the makeshift floor, he remembered the night when a young man had mercilessly killed his parents. Even after thirty years the pain was so harsh that he still felt moisture in his eyes. On umpteen times he had cursed himself of not having given Prabhas to the policeman when he hid in his cottage. Today as he saw the walls plastered with photos of Prabhas Shukla his mind went back in time and he wanted to take revenge.

A few days back Pappu had harvested the venoms from his snakes. The venom would fetch him good money since the two snakes he had were kraits. Pappu bandaged his right hand and taped a small syringe with a needle inside so that only the tip was protruding while the syringe was hidden below the bandage. He aspirated almost all the venom from the vial into the syringe. Once equipped, Pappu traversed the two hundred meters distance painfully using a walking stick up to the mansion of Prabhas Shukla. Already a long line had been formed leading from the gate of the mansion upto the car which was the official car of the CM. Pappu could see a long unending queue of cars both preceding and following the CM's official car. Pappu got a place at the end of the line of persons vying with each other for a glimpse of their new CM.

Prabhas Shukla, in all white, emerged from his mansion amidst deafening roar from the crowd. He passed the line of people paying obeisance. Frequently he would stop to say a word or pat someone. Almost at the end, Prabhas saw Pappu. He remembered this invalid beggar. Prabhas had a sharp memory and he instantly remembered that this beggar had given him a place to hide when the police had almost caught him. Prabhas bent and touched Pappu in a show of affection. Pappu with his right hand heavily bandaged caught Prabhas's feet and started weeping. Prabhas felt a sharp pain. In normal circumstances the result may have been different but the importance of the day and the sight of the weeping beggar prompted Prabhas to ignore the momentary discomfort. He moved on and sat in his car.

The caravan of cars moved instantly. Prabhas could see that people stood on both sides of the street. It was a dream come true. Five minutes into the journey, Prabhas felt a strange headache. As he tried to focus on the street ahead his eyes started giving him blurred images. He wanted the car to stop but found that no words were coming out from his mouth. His tongue was paralyzed.

The caravan reached its destination. A huge crowd was waiting to welcome the new CM. As the CM's car stopped, several people rushed to open the door. The door was opened. The crowd was stunned. The dead body of Prabhas Shukla lay motionless on the seat.

The city was aghast at the news of the death of the popular leader. All the loudspeakers were muted. On the banks of Yamuna River, on a raised stone structure, sat Pappu looking at the serenity of this majestic river which was perhaps the only witness to a ghastly twin murder of Suresh and his wife some thirty years back. What you sow comes back.

The Neighbour's Wife

On this first Monday of July, the day had started early for Manoj. Excited as he was, Manoj had taken his four-year-old son to his first day in the school. Returning to home on his two-wheeler, Manoj realised that it was going to be hectic today. He glanced at his watch and made a mental calculation how much time he had this morning to get ready, have breakfast and then again go to the ICICI bank where he worked. Without any effort to test his arithmetic, his mind told him that he better be fast. Just yesterday, the bank manager had circulated the terse notice that the photographic attendance would be sent to the ICICI head office at 9.45 am. Manoj realised it was futile to take any chances by being late to the bank. He accelerated. It was around eight when he touched home.

As Manoj completed his chores, Varsha was quick to make breakfast for Manoj. Taking a few bites on the way, Manoj rushed to the lift in the balcony of his third floor flat to go to the basement where his two-wheeler was parked. The Grand Towers was a high-rise apartment block having seven floors. It was only last month that Manoj had shifted to this new address. While going for the lift he passed by several people in the corridor but nobody seemed familiar. As Manoj descended to the basement floor, Manoj realised the vagaries of modern lifestyle. In this labyrinth of hundreds of flats in the same building, everybody was alone. Driven by an unknown sense of urgency every human behaved like a robot. The door of the lift opened and Manoj found his two-wheeler exactly at the same place where he had parked it.

As Manoj paced his bike on the inside road of his apartment's building his eyes caught sight of somebody he seemed to recognise. Just outside the entrance of the Grand Tower building, there was always a beeline of autorickshaws beckoning prospective passengers coming out from the apartment block during the rush office hour. In the melee of the jostling crowd, Manoj saw Jyoti. Jyoti was the girl who had joined ICICI Bank a few days back. In the last two days, Manoj had seen her sitting in the far corner but had got no opportunity to talk to her. Today while he navigated the crowded passageway of his building, he passed by her but didn't stop. Manoj glanced at his watch; it was already half passed nine. With a lingering image of Jyoti stored in the hippocampus region of his brain, Manoj took the road towards the ICICI bank, in five minutes he was in the bank.

Jyoti haggled with a couple of autorickshaws before she found a willing driver to take her to ICICI bank in Vikas Nagar area. She flipped her mobile and saw the time realising that she was already late by a few minutes. While the autorickshaw took the three-kilometer road, Jyoti's mind tried to decipher the fading memory of a motorcycle driver who had crossed her a few minutes back. She seemed to recognise the face but could not place it correctly. Once settled on the rikshaw her eighty-six billion neurons made another bid to find an answer and within a millisecond she recognised the person on the motorcycle. Although she did not know his name but her memory dictated that he was the Assistant Manager in the same branch of ICICI bank where she worked. It took Jyoti ten minutes to reach the bank. As she entered, she saw the attendance photo session in progress. Someone acknowledged Jyoti's presence and asked her to join after the first photo had been taken. Jyoti sheepishly stood as the last person in the row. A few places towards the middle stood the Assistant Manager whom she had seen on the motorcycle ten minutes before. Manoj saw Jyoti. His mind recollected the moment when he had passed her while she stood amidst the din searching for a rickshaw this morning. Manoj looked towards Jyoti, in that maroon sari, which signified the uniform of ICICI bank, she looked pretty. A streak of vermillion at the parting hair line on the forehead advertised the marital status.

While Manoj immersed into the work at his desk in the bank, his wife Varsha too felt heavy with work. Today she was expected to bring their son from the school at half past eleven. Varsha kept on watching the clock on the wall lest she lost count of the time. As if to add to her woes, the domestic help too came late. Despite the deluge of work, somehow, Varsha had managed to reach the school just in time. Being the first day of the new session, it was quite a rush. She returned home feeling exhausted at around noon.

While Manoj and Varsha's morning had started early this Monday, in the adjoining flat, Jyoti had silently made a cup of tea and kept in the microwave, before she had packed a sandwich for herself and had gone to her bank. Atul had woken only for the moment to say 'bye' and then had again gone to sleep. It was at around half past ten that his alarm had rang. Atul had taken another hour to get ready and left home at five minutes to noon to his undergarments shop situated in the downtown market.

Varsha alighted from the rickshaw and with her son in tow and headed straight for the lift. The lift displayed 'three'. She pushed the button for ascent and waited. The lift opened and a few people got out before Varsha could enter the cubicle. In the heat of the moment and the anxiety to reach home, she didn't realise that her mobile had slipped from her hand before she had entered the lift. The door closed and the lift started moving up.

As Atul stepped out of the lift, he noticed a pretty lady waiting just in front. Although she was followed by a small boy in school uniform, her countenance betrayed her marital status. Her pretty innocence was attractive. Without any obvious intent, Atul's eyes continued to follow the lady inside the lift until the door closed. It was while he turned towards the gate that Atul realised something had touched his feet. He looked down and found a phone on the floor. Bewildered he picked the phone, his mind wandering options what he should do. It was at this moment that the phone started ringing. Gingerly Atul hit the green dot. A startled feminine voice on the other side seemed relieved. The lady politely mentioned that she had lost her phone and would like to retrieve it. After a brief conversation, five minutes later, Atul found himself in front of a flat which was just adjacent to his own flat. The door opened and he came face-to-face once again with the pretty lady who had just a few minutes ago made an impression on his mind. During the conversation, Atul came to know that her name was Varsha and that her husband worked in the ICICI bank. As if her physical attributes were not sufficiently encouraging, Atul found that Varsha was also good in conversation. He could sense her glee when he told her that he had a shop in the main market selling women undergarments.

Within a few days Manoj got several opportunities to interact with Jyoti in the bank. When Manoj mentioned that he lived in the Grand Apartments, Jyoti interjected and told him that she knew this after having seen him in the Apartment's entrance several times. Manoj found Jyoti both affable and interesting. He started looking forward to the lunch break which provided him an opportunity to sit next to Jyoti and chat for a few moments.

It was a Friday morning, the last week of July, when it started to rain incessantly in the morning. Manoj didn't fancy riding the two-wheeler in that weather but he could not afford to take leave. Varsha advised him to take a rikshaw to the bank. In the adjacent flat, Jyoti was getting ready to go to the bank. She too was worried about the heavy downpour but had no option. An obscure thought made her think about Manoj, he also must be getting ready.

It was hard to keep the umbrella steady in that heavy downpour with high winds, Jyoti held the umbrella handle tight while using her other hand to keep her sari in place. It was during this commotion between heavy downpour, blowing wind, ground water puddles and milling rikshaws that Jyoti felt the presence of someone beside her which was beyond the limit of normal approach. To her surprise, she found Manoj standing beside her holding an old black umbrella. Her countenance suddenly changed from being apprehensive to inviting, she smiled. Manoj beckoned a rikshaw and showing no hesitation, as if ordained, Jyoti sat beside him. The rain came from all sides, the ill covered rickshaw provided very little protection to the two passengers. To shield herself from water seeping from the sides, Jyoti moved closer to middle. Manoj felt the warmth of Jyoti's body. A strange emotion overwhelmed Manoj, he looked towards Jyoti. It was at that very moment when Jyoti glanced towards Manoj, she saw a strange look in his eyes. Jyoti blushed, the rickshaw hit a pothole and jumped. Involuntarily Jyoti clutched Manoj's hands for support.

By the time Atul had woken up and dressed the rain had already lost its fury. A light drizzle made the weather brighter than what it was in the morning. Today being a Tuesday, Atul wanted to pay obeisance to Lord Hanuman and decided to visit the temple which was situated near the second street from Grand Towers. As Atul stood with folded hands in front of the deity, a passing shadow made him realise that someone known had just entered the temple. It is beyond human control to keep the mind shut even when engrossed in prayer. While Atul prayed reciting shlokas which he had learnt during childhood, his mind decoded the identity of the person who had followed him in the temple. Even before he had completed his prayer, Atul's mind told him that the silhouette which crossed him was Varsha, his next-door neighbour. Human brain is a wicked organ. Today, after having come to understand that Varsha was also praying and that she may still be in the temple for some more minutes, Atul deliberately decided to prolong his stay. While Atul's gesture would have been perceived by others as an extended show of reverence, Atul himself knew that he was indeed waiting for Varsha to complete her routine.

As Atul and Varsha walked back to Grand Towers from the temple, communication drifted from pleasantries to mundane. There were still quite a few puddles of water on the street after the morning downpour and it required an effort to navigate the walk. Suddenly Varsha tripped. Atul held her hand and gave her support. In that emergent situation, Varsha for a moment didn't realise that Atul's hand had firmly held her waist. Although the moment had lasted a few seconds, but somehow, both felt the lingering feeling of that benign touch. For a couple of minutes nobody spoke. The couple of minutes silence at this point of time was more eloquent than a two-hour romantic interlude. While Atul felt a heavenly joy recollecting the moment, Varsha felt a bit weird to realise that deep down in her instincts she had felt nice when Atul had touched her.

While Manoj sorted out files, he could see Jyoti at the far corner of the hall dealing with customers. Manoj joyfully allowed his mind to playback the events of this morning. He felt he could still sense the heat of Jyoti's body while she sat enticingly close fully drenched in that rickshaw. Jyoti felt reluctant to acknowledge that she too felt an amorous charm while she sat close to Manoj. During lunch, Jyoti offered Manoj half of the sandwich which she had brought. Manoj gleefully pushed a paratha from his tiffin into Jyoti's tiffin.

In the days, weeks and months that followed, getting up early and going to bank became a pleasant routine for Manoj. Almost everyday at around half past nine he would receive a message from Jeevan saying that 'I am ready'. Manoj understood this was the message from Jyoti. Within a couple of minutes of the message Manoj would take out his motorcycle from the basement, take the road and wait once outside the frame of sight from Grand Towers. A few seconds later Jyoti would join him and within eight minutes they would reach ICICI bank.

In the last few months, Atul had become an ardent Hanuman devotee. He would be ready soon after Jyoti left home and wait for a cryptic message on his phone. Invariably between eleven thirty and noon he would receive a message from someone named Varun saying that 'I am on my way'. Within minutes Atul would join Varsha on way to the temple.

Varsha noticed the pleasant change in Manoj's behaviour. Earlier Manoj would complain of fatigue after coming from the bank but now he was not complaining about workload and late hours. Even after returning, Varsha realised that Manoj spent large amount of time in talking on phone with friends, especially his new friend Jeevan. Just twenty yards from Varsha's flat, Jyoti also felt a change for the good in Atul's behaviour. She realised that of late Atul had become very religious. Even on days when she had the bank holiday, Atul would make it a point to visit the Hanuman temple and pay obeisance.

A hectic day was in progress in the ICICI bank. Manoj was deluged with work, suddenly he received a call from his Branch Manager. Calls from superior officers invariably spelt more work. As Manoj entered the Branch Manager's cabin, for a change he observed that the Manager was in a happy mood. The Manager told him that Manoj had been selected by the Head Office to go to Mumbai for the annual conference for a week. The conference was starting in ten days time. Returning to his desk, a slew of thoughts crossed his mind. Although spending ten days in Mumbai on bank's expense was exciting but then it also meant he would be away from home and especially Jyoti. While he chewed on the Mumbai visit, a thought struck. Could he try to take Jyoti along?

That evening, Manoj told Varsha about how he had been informed by the Manager to attend the conference at Mumbai. Later when Varsha was preparing dinner, she could overhear, Manoj was having a long conversation with his friend Jeewan. From the kitchen Varsha could understand that Manoj was coaxing Jeewan to accompany him to Mumbai. Varsha made a silent wish that Manoj may go with his friend Jeevan. Two men are likely to behave responsibly.

The next day when Manoj met Jyoti he discussed with her a plan. Jyoti would tell Atul that she was being sent to Mumbai by ICICI bank for a conference for ten days. If Atul agreed, she would take leave from the bank and accompany Manoj. The more they both thought about the plan the more feasible it seemed. That evening Jyoti told Atul the prepared script of her being selected for the bank conference. While Jyoti was telling Atul about the prospective dates of her Mumbai visit, Atul's mind was thinking of another plan.

The next day when Atul met Varsha during their temple visit, he told Varsha about Jyoti's Mumbai conference. Varsha nodded in agreement telling Atul that Manoj was also going to the same conference. Atul then floated the idea to Varsha of their own out of town journey during the time Jyoti would be away to Mumbai. That evening when Manoj came home, he told Varsha that his Mumbai trip was almost finalised and that he would be going on December 20th for ten days. The same evening Jyoti told Atul that she has received the final letter from the bank and she would be going to Mumbai on December 20th to attend the conference. That night Atul texted Varsha that Jyoti is finally going on December 20th and their plan would stand.

It was already December 18th, only two days were left. Manoj was making preparations, new clothes, shoes and bank papers. A few yards beyond the wall in the next flat another set of preparations were underway, this preparation also looked real except that Jyoti knew it was a sham. Jyoti's emphasis was more on clothes. In the last few days she had silently took out several new skimpy undergarments from the boxes which were kept to be sent to the shop.

On December 20th, Manoj called Uber for going to the airport for the Mumbai flight. Around the same time, an Ola received a message from Grand Tower to ferry a passenger to the airport. Atul escorted Jyoti to the waiting car. He held her hand and caressed it. As the Ola left the building, Atul waved a long goodbye.

After returning to his flat, Atul searched for Varun in his contacts and called. Today there was no need to be discreet. He had all the time to talk to Varsha. Atul told Varsha that Jyoti was expected to return by December 30th, and that they should make such a programme that their return should be a day before December 30th. Atul also proposed that Goa would be the best place to visit in December. As a mischievous afterthought, Atul told Varsha that he had selected several very sexy undergarments including a few bikinis for her Goa beach visit.

Varsha, albeit a bit scared, started to believe in Atul's proposed programme. Since the schools were going to be closed for the winter vacations, she decided to send her son to her parents' place. Prateek always enjoyed his stay when in the company of his maternal grandparents.

It was late in the evening when Atul called Varsha and told her that he had booked a hotel in Goa starting from December 24th and by tomorrow he would book the tickets. Later in the evening Manoj sent a whatsapp message to Varsha, laced with a heart emoji, informing that he had reached his hotel in Mumbai. In the neighbouring flat a similar message was received by Atul. In reply, Atul wrote 'miss U'.

Manoj had booked a different hotel from the one in which most of the other delegates of the conference were staying. Although the conference was starting from the next day, Manoj's thoughts were focused on the time he would spend with Jyoti. In that sheer gown, Jyoti looked tempting. Manoj ordered dinner in the room but didn't eat much. His thoughts were rivetted towards Jyoti. That night Jyoti didn't disappoint Manoj.

Manoj attended the conference in abstract mood, his mind was always thinking about Jyoti. Jyoti realised Manoj was so different from Atul. His energy and stamina were unsatiable. Both Manoj and Jyoti were enjoying this moment.

Varsha had sent her son to her parent's house with the added information that she would be visiting a friend in the nearby city for a few days. These days Atul needed no alibi to talk to Varsha. Just yesterday he had brought for her from his shop several choicest undergarments which could be classified more as a male delight than a woman's necessity. The necessary preparation were complete and Atul found the night of December 23rd unnecessary long. He longed for the moment when Varsha would be in his arms.

Atul and Varsha checked into the Hotel Cidade de Goa which was just ten minutes from Panjim downtown. The hotel exuded luxury. The room was elegantly decorated with windows facing the sea beach. As soon as the concierge had departed, Atul closed the door. He hugged Varsha. For the next half an hour it was total bliss. Exhausted, Atul ordered room service.

While Atul and Varsha soaked themselves in steamy endeavours, approximately six hundred kilometers away in Mumbai, the ICICI conference ended on December 26th, two days before its scheduled closure because the delegates wanted to go home for the New Year. Manoj felt cheated by the sudden change in the programme, he had planned to stay upto December 30th. In the night, contemplating options, Manoj came up with a suggestion that they both go to Goa for a couple of days before going back to their city.

The hotel managed their morning flight tickets to Goa and also booked their stay at the Hotel Cidade de Goa in Panjim. It was just after noon that Manoj and Jyoti checked into Cidade de Goa. The morning flight meant that their sleep was a bit curtailed. Whether it was a genuine sleep requirement or pure lust, Manoj found an excuse to hit the bed with Jyoti. It was after two hours that Manoj picked up the intercom to order room service.

Two days had passed but except for a brief evening walk on the beach, Atul and Varsha had confined themselves to the room and the bed. Since the return date was just a couple of days later, Jyoti suggested that they take a one-day tour of Goa's beaches. Manoj called reception and booked two seats in the tour bus of the hotel for the next day.

A similar decision was also being contemplated in the adjacent room # 209. Varsha wanted to visit the famed Goa beaches and called reception to seek travel assistance. The young lady at the reception advised Varsha that the hotel has a tour bus service which will go to all the tourist destinations and beaches. Varsha booked two seats for the next day.

Atul and Varsha had a quick breakfast and got ready for the bus tour. In the bag they kept towels, a set of slippers, water bottle and a spare dress. Relenting to Atul's insistence, Varsha agreed to wear the bikini under her rather skimpy gown. It was at dot eight in the morning when Atul and Varsha took their seat in the bus. There were four more couples on the bus. No one was making any effort to be modest.

The bus driver took his seat and inspected his passengers. One row of two seats was still empty. The driver gave a few horns. In room # 208, Manoj and Jyoti had slept late after a rather hectic night. It was already ten minutes past eight when they finally locked their room and rushed towards the bus which was standing at the gate.

Inside the bus, taking a cue from the unabashed behaviour of co-passengers, Atul and Varsha were locked in an embrace. Thus, they missed the moment when the new couple entered the bus and took their seat just opposite to their seat.

Jyoti looked around and froze. She saw Atul and Varsha in tight embrace locking lips. The very moment, a sixth sense prompted Atul that something was amiss. He released Varsha and turned towards right, his eyes locked straight into the bewildered face of Jyoti. The bus driver, oblivious to the comedy of lust being played out a few seats behind, started the bus. The other passengers were so preoccupied with their own partners that they failed to notice why the two couples seated on seats 2a, b and 2c and d, had become statues. Neither Atul nor Manoj could utter a word. In a slow motion, Varsha stood up from her seat and on cue Jyoti also stood from her seat. Varsha took a step and sat beside Manoj and Jyoti took the seat vacated by Varsha on the side of Atul. A few co-passengers who witnessed this changeover thought the two couples had agreed to wife swapping.

The Bangle Seller

His mother was caressing his forehead. Juned wanted to sleep more, the soft touch of the hand of his mother made his sleep become more intense. He heard his mother's voice calling his name and saying that tea was ready. Juned again felt his mother's hand stroking his forehead, he wanted to wake up but the deep sleep had immobilised his body. Juned again heard her mother calling him, however, this time the voice came from a distance. Juned opened his eyes and became abreast with the reality. He realised he was having a dream. Juned continued to stay put on his cot, he counted on his fingers, it had been thirty-two days since his mother had passed away after a brief illness. Juned continued to lie on the cot despite the clock on the front wall showing that it was already late in the morning. On usual days, when mother was alive, Juned would be ready to go to the college at ten in the morning. But things had changed in the last thirty-two days. His eyes became moist due to swelling tears, Juned again adjusted his pillow and closed his eyes.

It was at around one in the afternoon that Juned finally left his cot. He felt hungry. Despite the fact that Juned's parents had always lived a financially constrained life, Juned, being the only child to his doting parents, was constantly pampered. Today, while Juned put a pot of water on the gas to make tea, he realised that while his parents were alive, he was never required to do household chores. While the water took time to boil, Juned's mind took him to the memory of his late father who had passed away a couple of years back during the second COVID wave. Juned recollected that his father had a bangle shop in the main bazar. After his death, the shop had closed because the rent was getting accumulated. Juned's mother had started a small shop from her home selling bangles to the womenfolk in the locality. Juned's thoughts were broken when he saw that water was boiling. He made himself a cup of tea. It was while he sipped tea that Juned realised that he must look for options to earn money.

Late into that afternoon, Juned contemplated options for earning a living. Life, he realised, could be cruel without the umbrella of parents. In the last couple of weeks a few kind hearted souls in the locality had helped him with some money but he knew this was not a permanent solution. Even as his mind frantically explored different options, desperation crept in. Life had indeed not given him enough time to prepare for such a situation. Since his childhood, Juned had seen only bangles. Still two wall almirahs in his dingy home was occupied by bangles, some in soft cardboard boxes and some tied in twine. As much as he thought, all his thoughts ended in bangles. It was around midnight that Juned decided to explore his destiny by starting a business in bangles.

That Thursday night he found it difficult to sleep. The local mosque cleric had advised him to start the new business from Friday. Juned had already rented a hand cart on which he had arranged the bangles in heaps. There were bangles of all hues and colours, some even sequined. Remembering old conversations between his parents, Juned recollected those bangles came in different sizes and measured in inches according to diameter; 'two-one' and 'two-three' were the normal sizes, the larger sizes were 'two-six' and 'two-eight'. Juned kept changing his position but sleep was hard to come that Thursday night. It was sometime after three in the morning that Juned lost count of the time, his mind drifted to sleep. *His mother was stroking his forehead, her soft fingers went through his hairs, Juned heard his mother call him lovingly*. Juned opened his eyes, he realised he was dreaming. The wall clock showed it was eight in the morning. The dream had brought tears in his eyes but he ascribed a good omen to what he had seen in his dream, he thought that mother was happy with what Juned was going to do.

Juned had filled his cart with bangles and was about to embark on a journey which probably would define his life from now onwards. The one thing which he had not yet figured out was the place where he would sell his bangles. Aimlessly, Juned pushed his cart passing through lanes and by lanes, he found that selling bangles on a cart was a difficult preposition. It was well past the afternoon that he had his first customer. A couple of ladies stopped by his cart and asked him to show bangles. Hesitantly Juned marshalled all his courage not to show that he was a novice. The customer haggled but settled on a price. Juned had sold his first set of bangles.

Days progressed with Juned pushing his cart on uncharted lanes and streets. He slowly learnt the art of convincing customers and the guile of reading the mind before settling on a price. By the third day, Juned was earning enough to sustain his daily needs. Juned replenished his cart with new bangles.

In a couple of months, Juned had picked up the tricks of a street seller. He knew the best places where to park his cart and imbibed the acumen to escape the policemen who would come calling to extort money. His favourite spot was the trisection in the vicinity of the girls college. He had observed that college girls were not so fastidious, they also haggled less.

A year had passed and Juned became a master at selling bangles. He had a pulse for the latest fashion trends and got his bangles directly from manufactures in Mumbai, Surat and Firozabad. His cart became bigger, in a bid to cater to his growing feminine customer base, he started keeping a few boxes of cosmetics which complimented the array of bangles on offer.

It was the first Monday of April and the college had opened for the new session. There was a crowd of students, all girls, some excited, some forlorn and some bored portraying a look that they have been sent to college against their wishes. The college gave over at two in the afternoon and within a few minutes, Juned's cart was surrounded by girls. Some really interested in buying bangles and some just curious onlookers.

Juned scanned the teaming flock of girls surrounding his cart, the last couple of years had taught him the art of picking serious customers from reluctant ones. While his eyes scanned the customers that Monday afternoon, Juned's eyes caught sight of a beautiful girl in dark green top. There was something in her which was unknowingly attractive. As Juned's eyes lingered for an extra second on her face, she looked up meeting his gaze. Juned felt an emotion which was alien. While he catered to other customers, his eyes followed the damsel. He became aware that the girl was interested in red bangles and was in the process of selecting her choice. She took her time. When most of crowd had left his cart, Juned saw the girl come closer to him with two sets of bangles. She asked him which size would fit her. Juned gave a glance to her wrist and professionally told her that size two-three would fit her. The girl handed Juned the bangles she had selected and in an innocent tone asked him to put them in her hand. Juned's heart skipped a beat. As part of his profession, there have been occasions when he had facilitated women with wearing of bangles but when this girl requested, he found her gesture an alluring preposition. Gingerly he held her outstretched hand in his left hand and with his right hand slid the bangles in sets of three up her wrist. The dark red bangles looked angelic on those slender unblemished wrists. Juned glanced up; the girl had an innocent demeanor. Juned wished this moment could be frozen.

In the evening while Juned made dinner he overcooked his vegetables. Although he was sitting in front of the stove, he didn't realise that the vegetables had turned black. Juned realised he was thinking of the girl who had purchased red bangles that afternoon.

Days seemed longer to Juned after that Monday when he had met the girl who had purchased red bangles. Despite a healthy business all day, Juned's eyes kept scanning the crowd for someone. It was on the next Friday that Juned realised he had a visitor whose presence made him happy. The nameless girl was again fidgeting the displayed bangles. Juned saw her and at that very moment the girl looked up, Juned's gaze met her sight. Juned could discern a subdued smile on her face, in that maroon top she looked ethereal. Juned's eyes followed her. She did not purchase anything and left the cart. It was a good ten yards after she had walked away that she turned back and looked at Juned. Her eyes met Juned's line of vision. She smiled. This time her smile was genuine, Juned smiled back.

She didn't show up for the next few days. For the last many days Juned was less interested in selling than finding an excuse to meet that girl. On that Tuesday when Juned was aimlessly sitting on the stool beside his cart waiting for the time for the college to give over, he had a visitor. The time was odd since classes were on but Juned had a beautiful visitor. Juned displayed a wide grin. The girl also sported a happy countenance. Sometimes the mind goes blank when things happen unexpectedly. Juned experienced a feeling which made him look sheepish. The girl laughed seeing Juned fumbling for words. She came closer, looking directly at Juned she said 'my name is Zeba'. She turned back and walked to the gate of the college. While she was about to go out of sight, she turned back. She waived and entered the college. Juned continued to look in the direction for a couple of minutes after she had already gone.

Life changed for Juned henceforth. Selling bangles was no longer an arduous everyday affair. Every morning Juned looked forward to his rendezvous with Zeba. On occasions he would push a box of bangles in her hand without asking for any money. It was not long that Zeba asked Juned his name. Albeit discretely, Zeba would stop at the cart and exchange a few pleasantries while she came to the college and left in the afternoon.

Juned found out that much like him Zeba also didn't have surviving parents. She was living with her elder brother and his wife. Juned understood that Zeba had a lonely environment and she always had intra family niggles. It was not long that Zeba became a constant companion for Juned in thoughts.

On the professional front Juned was doing reasonably fine. In the last couple of years, he had purchased all the basic amenities at home. In recent months some distant relatives have also come calling with feelers for marriage. It was on a Sunday evening when Juned visited his maternal aunt in another locality that he opened up regarding his affection for Zeba. Events thereafter moved fast. Juned's aunt visited Zeba's home with a proposal for marriage. Zeba's brother and his wife seemed more than happy to accept the proposal. Since Juned had already stated that he was against any kind of dowry, the marriage was a low key affair. It was a Friday evening when after a short nikah ceremony, Juned brought Zeba to his house which was decked with Diwali lights. On that conjugal night, Juned took Zeba's hands and made her wear red bangles from elbow to wrist. The delicate henna tattooed hands looked enticingly beautiful. Zeba held both her hands together in front of her face, Juned softly held her hands and kissed her.

Zeba brought loads of luck for Juned. His bangles were much in demand. It was Ramazan time and the sales were high. Usually, the customers were mostly females but sometimes Juned saw a few male customers come to his cart to buy bangles with specific choices. At times he had young men who, as he thought, wanted to gift these to their girlfriends. It was a Monday afternoon and a brisk customer time when Juned saw a man in his fifties park his scooty nearby and walk to his cart. His appearance belied the regular set of customers who would come to Juned's cart. After getting an opening between the womenfolk crowding around the cart, the man, in a measured voice, asked Juned whether he had bangles in the size of 'two- eight'. Juned knew he did have a few bangles of that size but they were kept deep below the regular bangles and he did not want to waste time. Juned said 'no'. The man showed no reaction but asked whether Juned can get him those bangles tomorrow. The insistence of the customer gave the impression that he would really buy the bangles. Juned asked the man to come next day when the 'two - eight' bangles would be available. True to his words, the man again visited Juned's cart the next day. Juned found the choice of the bangles a bit weird, the 'two - eight' bangles were the biggest size available and they were sold on rare occasions. Expecting a bargain, Juned had adopted the habit of first telling a higher price which he would invariably reduce to give a psychological solace to the customer. To his amazement, the man took out his wallet and paid Juned the asking price without a hint of quibble. The man left as quietly as he had arrived.

Time passed for Juned with Zeba fully entrenched in her new home. In the couple of months she had made the two dingy rooms a decent place to live. On Sundays when Juned had a day off, he would take Zeba to parks and malls. Life was progressing smoothly. It was a Friday morning when Zeba complained of a bout of nausea, she felt uneasy and low. In the evening Juned visited the doctor and within minutes a beaming Juned emerged from the doctor's chamber with the news that Zeba was pregnant.

Pregnancy took a toll on Zeba's health. She became anemic and pale. The doctor advised her bed rest. The beginning of second trimester heralded new problems, Zeba found it difficult to attend to her chores, invariably she would feel heavy in arranging breakfast and lunch box for Juned. The absence of any elderly woman weighed heavily in the lives of Juned and Zeba. At times Juned would show displeasure to Zeba when he found her skipping mundane tasks. It was a Monday morning when Zeba slept unusually late, when she woke Juned was already ready. Zeba hurriedly started making breakfast but Juned didn't wait for her. Showing strong displeasure, he left without breakfast or lunch box.

It was the first time in the last six months, after marriage, that Zeba wept. She wanted to share her feelings with someone but realised she had no one to lean. Her brother along with his family had gone to Saudi Arabia for greener pastures. That afternoon Zeba cooked many things which in her opinion were Juned's favourites. Although she was feeling tired she stood at the door waiting for Juned in the evening. Juned returned a full one hour late than his usual time. Zeba did her best to create a happy environment but realised that Juned was still stiff in attitude.

The doctor advised a note of caution while Zeba entered her seventh month. Despite gaining weight she looked frail. Her face looked a far cry from the time she would ogle at bangles keeping an eye on the handsome looking boy standing in front of the cart. During the long hours she spent at home, while Juned went out with his cart, Zeba would fondly reminisce the days when she would go to college. She remembered the first day when she had brought the red bangles from the cart stationed outside the college gate. An involuntary smile crossed her lips when she remembered how one day she had bunked her class and reached Juned's cart in an effort to meet him alone. Her mind brought back the adrenaline rush which she felt when she had found courage to tell her name to Juned. Zeba realised she had tears in her eyes. She looked at the wall clock, it was three in the afternoon, a good five hours for Juned to return.

July heralded the onset of monsoon, Juned had put a double layer of plastic on top of his cart. Monsoon was a dry month as far as sales were concerned. Few people, especially women, would venture out to buy bangles. Engrossed in his mobile, Juned sat on a plastic stool near his cart. Without looking up, he realised someone was standing on the other side of the cart. Juned looked towards the person, he recognised. The man had purchased the big size red bangles from his cart a few months back. In acknowledgement of his customer's age, Juned nodded a greeting. The man asked him whether he had green bangles of the size 'two - eight'. Fearing that a negative answer would cause disappointment, Juned dug deep in his cart and finally found a twine which had green bangles. The man asked for two dozen bangles and paid the price without any second thought. Juned saw that the man had braved rain to come to his cart, he was fully wet. Juned's mind drifted to the thought wherein he contemplated about the lady for which this man had braved the rain to buy green bangles on this first Monday of 'sawan'.

It was a Sunday morning when Zeba complained of cramps. She was full time and Juned rushed her to the hospital. Zeba remained in labour for almost eight hours, at five in the evening, a nurse with a professional smile informed Juned that Zeba had given birth to a baby girl and that both the mother and child were well. Two days later, Juned hired an Ola taxi to take Zeba and the newborn to his home.

If Zeba had found doing household chores difficult during pregnancy, the situation after childbirth became worse. She had constant pain in her lower abdomen and back. The constant attention to her child drained her strength. In addition to her medical constraints, Zeba found Juned showing less attention to her and to the child. He usually remained to himself. His humour and romance seemed to dry up after childbirth.

In the next few months, while a convalescing Zeba did her best to divide her time between her new born and everyday work, Juned became recluse. He spoke little and would often return late. Zeba observed that Juned frequently found an excuse to sleep alone in the other room. Zeba felt forlorn and depressed.

The child had been restless for most of the night and Zeba had been awake. It was around four in the morning that the child slept and Zeba also got time to close her eyes. When Juned woke up at seven in the morning he found Zeba and the child sleeping. Juned felt anger, he yelled at Zeba. The tired body already famished from breastfeeding took time to come to senses, Zeba didn't realise it was already time for Juned to start preparing his cart for the day. Juned yelled again, in a rage he moved menacingly towards Zeba but stopped just short of hitting her. This was the first time Zeba heard Juned use expletives.

Juned had parked his cart at the designated place. For last few days the sale has been less than normal. The afternoon was now not that hot as it was a month back. The soft November breeze laced with a scent of winter made a beautiful day although Juned, still angry with the attitude of Zeba, remained oblivious to the weather. Deep in his thoughts, Juned missed the sound of the scooty which had just stopped by his cart. He recognised the man. Pleasantries were exchanged. The man wanted golden bangles this time. Quite unexpectedly, Juned popped a question. He asked the man to bring his wife to his cart so that she can buy the bangles herself. Juned informed the customer that it was only for him that he had started keeping a full colour range of bangles for the size 'two - eight'. Juned saw the man smile. His eyes portrayed a glint of happiness. The man replied that he will bring his wife the coming Saturday. Juned felt jealous of the man, he thought what a lovely family this man must be having. Even at this age the man was buying bangles for his wife with so much affection.

Zeba was preparing breakfast when the child started crying. Juned was in the bathroom getting ready for today. Zeba attended to her child who seemed to be having a fever. When Juned came reaching for breakfast, it was still not ready. Juned's temper already on a high from a last night squabble, rose further. He started yelling and, in a fit, used his hands to slap the face of Zeba. He barged out of his house using cuss words against Zeba's parents.

Juned parked his cart and took out his stool. He was cursing himself for having married Zeba. Some customers came but Juned didn't make an effort to sell his bangles. It was at around two in the afternoon that a rikshaw came and stopped beside the cart. Juned saw the man, the recognised the man who had previously come on a scooty to buy big sized bangles, alight from the rikshaw. The man was helping someone else to come out of rikshaw. A woman with dark glasses emerged from the rikshaw, she was carrying a walking stick. The man helped her stand using the stick and guided her up to the cart. The woman looked visually challenged and wore a crumpled sari. Juned stood dazed to see the blind woman use her hand to feel the cart and the bangles. The man who had escorted the woman proudly told Juned that she was his wife and it was for her that he had bought all the bangles. While the couple talked within themselves, the man handed bangles to the woman who was using both her hands to feel the bangles. Juned stood dazed. The beautiful face of Zeba flashed before his eyes. He remembered the night when Zeba, hands full of coloured bangles, had given her body to him. While Juned's mind went through a kaleidoscope of thoughts, he missed the fondness which was transpiring between the middle-aged couple while the man selected an assortment of bangles for his blind wife.

Long after Juned had gone with his cart, Zeba continued to weep. For a brief moment she fainted. Her mind drifted to thoughts swinging from running away to suicide. She remembered her mother who had passed away while she was still in school. Despite the fact that she had no alternatives, she was convinced that it was difficult to remain in this house with Juned. The desperation grew stronger as time passed. She wanted to run away knowing fully well that she had no clear destination. It was five in the evening when finally, Zeba took her child in her lap and went out of Juned's house. She left the door unlocked.

The man and his blind wife bought several dozens of bangles. They paid without haggling and took the rikshaw. Juned's mind was experiencing a storm of emotions. The blind customer who had just purchased bangles had opened his eyes. Juned realised that a happy life is beyond material things and beauty. Even as evening descended, he could not make his mind wriggle out from thoughts of Zeba. For an umpteenth time he regretted his behaviour towards his wife. With tears in his eyes and a lump in his throat Juned packed his cart early and started back home. At a corner he came across the florist from where he bought a bunch of flowers. He stopped again at the bakery to buy a cake. Today he wanted to reach his beloved wife as fast as possible.

Zeba walked through unknown streets. Her mind was clouded with a thousand thoughts. She remembered the good times she had spent with Juned. Her mind meandered to those days when she would make it a point to wait for Juned at the door while he returned from work. She also remembered that Juned was invariably very hungry when he returned and that he would instantly ask for food. Zeba thought that despite his rude behaviour this morning, for which she had already taken the extreme step of leaving home, today Juned would find nothing to eat when he would return.

From a far mosque Zeba heard a *muezzin* call the *azan.* Her mind again reminded her that Juned must be packing his cart at this moment. In an unexplained gesture she turned back, with hurried steps she went back to home, the door was open as she had left it. Zeba wanted to prepare something for Juned to eat when he came back. She resolved that after preparing the meal she would leave the home for good. It was still an hour from the time she expected Juned to return back home.

Juned tip toed inside the house, Zeba did not hear Juned come inside, her mind was still too confused. She wanted to leave the house before Juned came. Juned hugged Zeba from behind. A startled Zeba shrieked at the touch. In that tight embrace Juned put the flowers in her lap. Zeba's tear laden eyes saw the remorse in Juned's eyes. Juned kissed her in the same way as he had done on the conjugal night.

The Second Love

Everything was as usual; she entered the hostel gate on her scooty as she had been doing for the past seven years. She knew each brick on the narrow path to the hostel premises, her scooty would navigate this distance even on autopilot. She reached her room, parked the scooty and unlocked the door. She looked at the upheaval on the bed and the dirty utensils stacked in the corner. Ignoring the chaos, Sunaina felt tired. She kicked her shoes and jumped onto the bed. Closing her eyes, she realised she was feeling drained. She closed her eyes and contemplated the events of the day.

Today she had woken up early, in fact, she recollected that she had hardly slept last night, she had prepared for her Ph. D. viva voce examination going through her powerpoint presentation several times. Sunaina realised she didn't remember the exact sequence of how her presentation unfolded. She only remembered the moment when she had heard the claps of other research scholars. She did remember the moment when her supervisor had congratulated her. This moment was surprisingly vividly frozen in her mind. She let her mind stop with the image of her supervisor.

Sunaina continued to lie in bed, it was already dinner time but she was in no mood to go to the mess. Her mind continued to play several moments of her seven years stay in the University during which she had completed her Master's and Ph.D. There were moments of both joy and despair in her mind's memory arsenal. At this point when she realised that her academic journey was going to end, she felt no remorse for all those moments which had given her pain. She realised that even the painful moments had some kind of latent joy. It was during this cinematic flashback of thoughts her mind suddenly stopped once again when a memory of her supervisor suddenly came in front of her eyes. It was today that she felt how much an influence he had had on her personality. Sunaina rubbed her eyes which were now moist with tears. She found it hard to decide whether those tears were of joy or sadness. Sunaina lazily stayed in bed when her mind played back the kaleidoscope of her memoirs, accumulated in her brain while she had traversed the life's journey from an adolescent to a young woman. Her thoughts were jolted when her phone rang. Sunaina understood her folly even before she had seen the name of the caller. In the journey of her thoughts, she had forgotten to call her parents.

It was her father who talked to her in the beginning. If indeed her father was not happy with Sunaina for not calling them when she had come back, he didn't show any anger. Mr Das doted on his daughter and today was a proud moment for him. He didn't talk much except congratulating Sunaina on her determination to complete her Ph D. In the couple of minutes that he spoke, it was hard for him to control his emotions. Sunaina felt the emotional tremble in her father's voice while he spoke on the phone. She too felt weak in the knees. Mr Das handed the phone to his wife. Sunaina's mother started by congratulating her daughter but she didn't mince words when she commanded her daughter to give a serious thought to all the marriage proposals she had been sending to her ever since she had completed her thesis. Sunaina heard the volley of instructions from her mother without saying a word. It was after a five-minute monologue that her mother closed the conversation.

Sunaina continued to remain in bed but her thoughts changed abruptly. The events of the day and the successful culmination of her Ph. D. defense found a place in a far recess of her brain. Her thoughts catapulted her to the trailing WhatsApp conversation which was going on between her and her parents for the last couple of months. Since the day she had submitted her Ph. D. thesis, her mother had been pestering her to go through the matrimonial recommendations which she was continuously forwarding for Sunaina to see. On her part, Sunaina had till now used the excuse of her pending Ph. D. viva voce examination to wriggle out of difficult decisions but this evening she understood the tone of her mother's conversation. Sunaina, resigned to reality, knew she had to commit to the pressures of nature's evolutionary design. She remembered a lecture of her supervisor where he had explained how every living system must procreate fulfilling the Darwinian purpose of life. Sunaina picked up her phone and scrolled the messages sent by her mother which included names and biodata of two boys whose parents had shown willingness to Sunaina's profile on the matrimony site.

Rakesh Raj's profile had all the ingredients of an eligible bachelor. His biodata exclaimed that after completing B.A.(Hons) from St. Xavier's College, Kolkata he had done MBA from Indian Institute of Management, Kolkata. Presently, Rakesh was an executive with the Federal Bank posted in New Delhi. There were two photographs that accompanied his profile. One was a long shot from a foreign location and the other was a close-up bust view. The face did not excite Sunaina's eyes but viewed in conjunction with the next entry on the biodata, his personality looked good. The biodata mentioned that Rakesh was getting a per annum package of Rs 80 lacs.

Sunaina closed her eyes and tried to visualise her life when she would be married. Her last seven years in the hostel had made her an independent bird. She had become habituated to late night movies and web series. She would habitually sleep till late mornings and would seldom cook. She realised that in the last couple of years she also did not want to go home during summer vacations. Marriage and that too in Indian scenario was akin to a dignified prison for the female. Sunaina had listened to several tales of her seniors about the restrictions imposed by in-laws. She shuddered. Sunaina's mind was cooking up hallucinations of a demon trying to kill her. The phone slipped out of her hand and her eyes drooped. She fell asleep.

It was at around ten in the morning that a dreary eyed Sunaina again continued her tryst with the mate selection exercise dictated by the options provided by her mother. She opened the second matrimonial profile in the WhatsApp message of her mother. Sudhir Majumdar's biodata did not start from the usual academic qualifications. It started with hobbies. Sunaina found this approach to life rather strange but infectious. The first three lines on the biodata detailed the hobbies which included music, reading English classics, Chess, Cricket and evolutionary biology. Lower down on his biodata there was a mention of Ph. D. in Economics. Way down it was mentioned that Sudhir was a Chartered Accountant by Profession and worked privately having an office in New Delhi. As an attachment to this word document was a photograph of a young man laughing his heart out with an ice cream in one hand. Sunaina realised that by the time she was done with the one-page biodata, she was smiling.

In the weeks that followed, Sunaina got the necessary clearances from the University and vacated the hostel room. For logistical reasons her parents had suggested that she go to New Delhi to live with her aunt for some time. Sunaina found the pampered stay in her aunt's house dull and boring. The care and the attention went against the idea of free will to which Sunaina had become so accustomed in her hostel life. Everyday her mother would call and coax Sunaina to decide on the matrimonial suggestions. Her mother provided Sunaina the phone numbers of both Rakesh Raj and Sudhir Majumdar and prodded her to start WhatsApp conversation in an effort to see who suited her best. As part of their recommendation, Sunaina's parents were too much inclined towards Rakesh. They wanted Sunaina to somehow accept their suggestion but didn't want to be dictating their choice.

It was eight in the evening when Sunaina mustered the courage to say 'hi' to Rakesh Raj on WhatsApp, signing off with 'I am Sunaina'. Her heart beat a bit faster. In the last seven years that she spent in the University, she had many male friends and Sunaina never felt awkward or intimidated in one-to-one conversations, but this experience was different. Sunaina was embarking on an uncharted territory.

What started as a benign 'hi' had culminated into a daily routine within fifteen days. Thus, Sunaina felt no hesitation to say 'yes' when

Rakesh implored her for a dinner date at the Taj Palace. With her adrenaline in overdrive, Sunaina met Rakesh on a reserved table. With all those lengthy WhatsApp chats behind her, Sunaina didn't find it difficult to engage Rakesh in conversation. The food, the ambience and the setting all exuded opulence but Sunaina found Rakesh a bit dull in showing male derived dominance, a hallmark of nature's mate selection strategy. He seldom laughed. In between dinner there were at least a couple of moments when he excused Sunaina for urgent business calls. While Sunaina and Rakesh walked back to the car, Sunaina's dress caught a pebble and she stumbled. In reflex action Rakesh held Sunaina's hand but swiftly released it as if he had done something wrong. A feeble 'sorry' escaped his lips. Sunaina found this attitude a bit weird.

In the next few weeks, Rakesh took Sunaina out for dinners regularly in some of the most happening places in Delhi. Almost invariably Rakesh would bring expensive gifts. Sunaina felt impressed with the show of affluence. On several occasions when her mother asked her on phone regarding Rakesh, Sunaina would invariably talk about the lavish and extravagant lifestyle of Rakesh. Since her parents were more than willing to accept Rakesh, Sunaina's silent admiration of Rakesh's wealth was construed as a silent yes to the marriage proposal.

While her parents were pretty delighted to sense that Sunaina was happy with Rakesh, Sunaina spent hours contemplating a life with Rakesh. Despite the exuberance of money which Rakesh never shied in flaunting, Sunaina felt a sense of void when she tried to connect emotionally with Rakesh. It was during a pensive moment that Sunaina remembered her mother had sent her two matrimonial references; she also remembered the interesting biodata of Sudhir who was a Chartered Accountant. Without giving it a reasoned thought, on an impulse, Sunaina sent a 'hi, Sunaina here' message in Sudhir's WhatsApp number.

Sunaina received a reply within five minutes. Sunaina noticed that in his reply Sudhir had introduced himself but had also added a small heart emoji after the message. Even on the first day, their WhatsApp conversation lasted forty-five minutes. Sunaina took note that Sudhir was very eloquent and his conversation was frequently laced with humour.

Sunaina slept late that Sunday. When she woke up, she saw a message from Sudhir. He had sent a 'Good morning' message. It was just after five minutes when Sunaina had got online that she received a call. It was Sudhir. Sunaina was not prepared to talk to Sudhir but on a strange impulsive instinct she hit the receive button. Sudhir's way of greeting brought smile on Sunaina's face. In between the evolving conversation Sudhir mentioned that for the last one hour or so he was constantly waiting to see when Sunaina would come online. What innocuously started as a greeting conversation lasted for half an hour. Sunaina felt fresh after talking to Sudhir. She realised his humour was infectious.

Within two days, Sudhir had called Sunaina half a dozen times. They met on a dinner date in a bistro. From the time Sunaina met Sudhir, she was floored by Sudhir's conversation. While the food was simple, Sunaina feasted upon a deluge of topics ranging from nuances of Indian classical music and the fascinating tale of Ernest Hemingway's ' The Old Man and the Sea'. While Sunaina listened dumbstruck, Sudhir opened new topics which were always better than the last one. Sunaina didn't realize she had spent two hours. She certainly didn't pay any attention to what was ordered or what she was eating. After dinner Sudhir came up with the idea that they both take a stroll in the Connaught Place before going home. They walked; Sunaina understood the intent but felt too feeble to protest when Sudhir put a hand around her waist. Sunaina walked the next fifteen minutes without listening to what Sudhir was saying. She was on cloud nine.

While Sunaina was on cloud nine, her parents were already in conversation with Rakesh's family regarding the marriage proposal. Rakesh's parents had informed Mr Das that Rakesh was going to London in two weeks' time and they wanted an early marriage.

While Sunaina's father tried to ask for more time to complete the preparations, Rakesh's father told him that they will book the Taj Palace Hotel and all preparations would be outsourced. Thus, time was not a hurdle.

Sunaina again could not protest when Sudhir called her the next morning and wanted her to accompany him for dinner. Tonight, they selected a non-decrepit downtown café. The food was simple but as usual Sudhir was mesmerizing. Sunaina felt a resonance of Sudhir's ebullience. After dinner Sudhir offered to drop Sunaina to her home. Already hypnotised with the wit of Sudhir, Sunaina meekly sat with Sudhir in his car. The intensity of emotions was such that despite the fear of being late to home Sunaina didn't want this journey to finish. Intoxicated with romantic thoughts, Sunaina made no protest when Sudhir took Sunaina to his flat. It was one hour later that Sudhir dropped Sunaina to her home. Sunaina was convinced. Sudhir was the man she wanted to spend the rest of her life. She decided she would convey this decision to her parents tomorrow.

It was late at night when Sunaina got a call from her father. Mr. Das informed her that they would be reaching New Delhi tomorrow by the morning flight. Sunaina was clueless as to the reason for this urgent programme of their parents. For a moment she tried to think about it but then she saw the 'Good night' WhatsApp message on her phone from Sudhir and her thoughts meandered to the evening spent with Sudhir which included a visit to his flat. A far voice in her mind cautioned her that she had already embarked too far in relationship with Sudhir without the consent of her parents but another voice made a convincing statement that everything was fine if she was indeed going to marry Sudhir. Sunaina lay confused. Her mind continuously brought back the images of Sudhir. He was certainly affable.

Sunaina's parents arrived with an unusual load of baggage. Her mother was brimming with joy when she embraced Sunaina in an emotional hug. Mr Das stood at a distance savouring the beautiful bonding between a mother and her daughter. Sunaina was perplexed;

she had no clue to explain the sudden exuberance of emotional display by her parents. Sensing Sunaina's blank countenance, her mother broke the ice. In an excited tone she whispered that they have conveyed to Rakesh's family that Sunaina is happy with the proposal. While Sunaina fought hard to control tears, her mother, oblivious to Sunaina's thoughts continued that as per Rakesh's London programme, it has been decided that the marriage will be solemnised on the next Sunday, a week from now.

The atmosphere in the house became lively. Sunaina's mother and her aunt helped each other with the sweets which Mr Das had brought. No one took any notice when Sunaina silently slipped to her room, her face fighting to restrain a plethora of emotions. With tears forming a convex covering upon her eyes, she glanced at her mobile which displayed three missed calls. All from Sudhir.

From now onwards there was no difference between day and night in the Das household. Preparations for the wedding extended to wee hours of the night. Rakesh had hired a leading costume designer for the wedding dress. The stitching team had visited Sunaina for exact measurements. Everything was so smooth; Sunaina had no option but to float with the flow. She ignored messages and calls from Sudhir. On Tuesday, finally, she blocked Sudhir.

The wedding was a surreal event. Mr Das and his close family were just bystanders in that grand show of opulence at the lawns of the Taj Palace. In a gown which flowed several feet behind Sunaina, the bride could be mistaken for a fairy. Rakesh walked with Sunaina under the instructions of the cameramen in attendance.

The fairytale marriage and the equally extravagant post-marriage parties left Sunaina with no time to think about any past events. Even without any obvious work, she was always felt preoccupied. Most of the parties which Sunaina attended were boring to her. She could sense the emotionless hypocrisy of the guests with most invitees sporting plastic smiles.

Time is a big leveler and soon Sunaina adjusted to the life in the fast lane. Rakesh would pamper Sunaina with gifts. It was to everyone's joy when Rakesh announced to his family that Sunaina was expecting. If indeed there was any respite from the constant adulation that Sunaina was already getting, after the news of pregnancy she was further pampered. Time moved fast, whether it was extra care or a miscalculation, Sunaina delivered a male child, a full one month premature.

Years passed in the life of Sunaina. In the hierarchy of successful entrepreneurs, Rakesh moved to the top rung. The meteoric rise of Rakesh meant that he had even less time for Sunaina and Amol who was now ten years old. Even at the young age, Amol was excelling in extracurricular activities. His interests were fascinating. He would spend hours watching scientific documentaries. On a trip abroad, Sunaina bought Amol a chess board and pieces. Within months, Amol was deep in chess shadow playing the highly documented games between the legendary Bobby Fischer and Boris Spassky.

Rakesh made it a point to be at home on the occasion of Amol's fifteenth birthday. A big party had been planned for the evening with invites having been extended to the city's glitterati. It was a rare occasion when Rakesh had opted to spend the full day with his family. It was forenoon and Rakesh affectionately beckoned his son to come to his first-floor office. The first-floor office was a place where normally no one entered. Even Sunaina, as an unsaid tradition, would seldom venture into that room. Affectionately Rakesh seated Amol on a chair next to his and showed him certain documents explaining the importance of each with respect to the wide portfolio of investments he had made. Amol listened to his father with rapt attention. Rakesh then showed Amol the secret vault and the place of the key. For a moment Rakesh opened the vault and showed Amol what was inside. Rakesh and Amol returned to the family room in twenty-five minutes.

The birthday party was a grand affair. Rakesh made it a point to meet each of his guests and also to introduce Amol. A giant fifteen layered cake was cut by Amol under the watchful eyes of Sunaina and Rakesh. The last of the guests left by eleven in the night. Sunaina was tired and so was Rakesh, although he didn't show it. It had been several years since Rakesh slept alone in his room, this practice started ostensibly on the pretext that he would do late night phone calls and chat with friends from across the globe. Sunaina and Amol always slept together.

Rakesh was an early riser. Invariably he would always wake up at five in the morning and go for a morning walk. Sunaina and Amol slept late. Today Sunaina and Amol slept extra late. Sunaina woke up at nine and went outside. She noticed that Rakesh's room was still closed. She opened the door a few centimeters and peeped. Rakesh was still asleep. She tiptoed to his bedside and put a hand on his exposed shoulder. Rakesh didn't respond. She called him by name. A loud shriek escaped Sunaina's lips. Rakesh was still and cold. She realised what had happened. Frenzy broke out in the house; within eight minutes the family doctor examined Rakesh and pronounced him dead.

Sunaina had no training how to handle matters of the corporate world. Rakesh would never speak about his business ventures and Sunaina on her part felt happy to be far from the complex world of balance sheets and international value of stocks.

It had been more than three months since Rakesh's death. The first couple of months had been tough for Sunaina with frequent emotional breakdowns every time she saw something connected with Rakesh, but time again provided the healing touch. After three months she had almost reconciled to the loss of Rakesh. It was just after a religious prayer meeting that Sunaina decided to pick up financial threads and understand the vast business ventures of Rakesh. Easier said than done, Sunaina realised this was hard. A friend counseled her to seek professional help.

On the advice from a close family well-wisher, Sunaina walked into the offices of ORCHID Investment Consultants. Sunaina was ushered into a waiting area. It was a good thirty-five minutes later that Sunaina walked into the wood paneled office of the Chief Consultant. The gold embossed name plate on the mahogany door read: Sudhir Mazumdar. Being lost in her own thoughts, Sunaina did not pay heed to the name and gingerly stepped inside the room. The man seated on the upholstered chair was fidgeting his drawer. While Sunaina stood across the table waiting for an invitation to sit down the man turned towards her and looked at her. Sudhir opened his mouth but could not say anything. His heart skipped a beat. Sunaina felt a rush of adrenaline when she saw Sudhir. She felt clueless as to what she should do. A kaleidoscope of thoughts came to her mind. With a transfixed gaze she stood motionless keeping her hands on the table, a gesture probably dictated by the momentary giddiness that engulfed her.

Sudhir gained composure and politely asked Sunaina to take a seat. Despite having an experience of fifteen years in this trade where public dealing is the norm, Sudhir fumbled for words to start a conversation. He said 'hello'.

Sunaina felt awkward to meet Sudhir's eyes. A silent tear slipped on to her cheek. She choked. Sudhir offered her water and took control of the situation asking Sunaina what was the problem. It took Sunaina more than an hour to tell Sudhir about Rakesh's untimely death and her ignorance of business ventures. Sudhir took the papers which Sunaina had brought and personally escorted Sunaina up to the outer gate.

Sunaina returned home in a state of mental riot. She blamed destiny for this chance encounter with Sudhir. In the last sixteen years she had forgotten Sudhir. As she lay down on the bed with Amol on her side, her mind played back and forth the moments when she first saw Sudhir in his office. A distant memory made her realise that Sudhir had not changed much. Despite a few specs of grey hair and a few extra kilos, Sudhir looked much the same. Despite making a conscious effort to stop the flow of old memories, her mind somehow reminded her that Sudhir was still good at talking.

Sudhir was still clueless how to explain this chance meeting with Sunaina. He too found destiny an alibi to interpret this new development. Sudhir realised that despite so much upheaval in life, Sunaina still had that latent charm which she exuded when they dated almost sixteen years back.

There were several more meetings of Sunaina with Sudhir in the next fifteen days. After a couple of subdued interactions, Sunaina started feeling comfortable while talking to Sudhir. At times, out of curiosity, she tried to explore Sudhir's personal life. Without assigning a reason, Sudhir told her that he didn't marry. To make further financial assessment, Sudhir asked Sunaina to bring some more papers. Sunaina had no idea which papers were required and invited Sudhir to her house to have a look in Rakesh's office.

It was a Sunday when the bell rang at four in the evening while Sunaina was playing chess with Amol. With a latent glee Sunaina welcomed Sudhir. Over a conversation which extended for almost an hour, Sunaina showed all the papers to Sudhir. While Sudhir chatted with Sunaina in his characteristic indominatable style, Amol watched with an apprehensive intent. At fifteen years of age, he was well grown up to recognise human emotions.

The next couple of months saw some frequent visits of Sudhir to Sunaina's house. In the last few months Sunaina had started looking forward to Sunday afternoons when Sudhir would visit. On his part, Sudhir too felt a rising urge to visit Sunaina on lame pretexts of looking at documents which probably had no relevance. There were numerous occasions when Sudhir would delve into topics which would elicit uncontrolled laughter from Sunaina. While her mother hosted Sudhir with usual cheerfulness, Amol felt a sense of betrayal. He abhorred Sudhir for the simple reason that a basic instinct in his mind prompted him that this friendship of his mother was not proper.

It was a Sunday afternoon when Sudhir reached Sunaina's house. Sunaina was already looking forward to his visit. The conversation today drifted to some past memories. Out of nowhere, Sudhir popped the question asking Sunaina why did she suddenly leave him without any reason. Sunaina didn't answer at first but her countenance showed that she wanted to say something. After a silent interlude Sudhir again asked the same question. Sunaina couldn't control herself. It took her a full twenty minutes, amidst incessant tears, to tell the full story to Sudhir.

Sudhir stood from his chair and walked towards Sunaina, he extended his hands and embraced Sunaina.

Amol had been away this afternoon playing football. As he returned home to an open front door, his eyes caught sight of his mother in tight embrace with Sudhir. Amol looked aghast; he remembered his father. Without waiting in the lobby, he ran up the stairs and went inside the first-floor office of his father. He opened the vault and ran down the stairs. Sunaina and Sudhir were still in tight embrace. He could see Sudhir caressing his mother's hair. Amol pointed the pistol towards Sudhir and fired. The bullet caught Sudhir on the left shoulder blade. He fell down. While Sudhir collapsed, a shriek escaped Sunaina's throat. She saw her son with the pistol.

Sunaina looked at the lifeless body lying next to her feet. She yelled at her son "what have you done Amol, you have killed your father".

A night with a damsel

Before I move onto the next story I would like to make a brief introduction. This story was written by my father (Late Agha Rizvi) sometime around 1973. In those days getting a printing platform and then advertising written works was a herculean job. My father expired in 2017, and one day while I leafed through his files and papers, I found this story.

My father, Late Agha Rizvi, had a decent Government job for a living but was more famous for his exploits on the cricket field. For several years he played Ranji Trophy for Uttar Pradesh and later was a selector of the State Team. Other than cricket he had interest in Indian classical music, Bridge (was a national champion), and chess. Last but not the least, for many years he was into sports journalism writing columns for newspapers. He also published a book "The Ancient Olympic Games".

The story: **A night with a damsel**, is based on his cricketing memories with an interesting twist.

The story starts from the next page.

A night with a damsel

With now mellowing in years, I find myself less hesitant now in sharing with others what I would have otherwise kept a closely guarded secret, say, about a decade ago. I might not have considered it worthwhile divulging to others, incidents which have absolutely no bearing now and as a result of little consequence.

The 1957-58 cricket season had been a very significant one for more than one reason. That was the year of 'away series' for Uttar Pradesh Ranji Trophy fixtures and in our second encounter we were pitched against Madhya Pradesh at Indore. Indore, having seen great cricketing giants turning out for Holkar in the past, usually attracted very few spectators in an ordinary Ranji match. But the match I am talking about did attract a sizable crowd presumably because of the presence of Vijay Manjrekar and C S Nayudu in our ranks and the Madhya Pradesh team fielding stalwarts like Mushtaq Ali, Sarwate, Jagdale, Hiralal Gaekwad and others.

Using superlatives for one's own self smacks of conceit and arrogance; but to give you a fair idea of what happened there in the middle of the Yashwant Rao ground that day. I shall have to shake off false modesty for a moment.

To say that I batted magnificently would be the understatement of the year. A description somewhat nearer to reality would be that I literally enthralled and regaled the crowd with my superb batting. Cutting to ribbons whatever attack was dished out, I treated the rival bowlers rather unceremoniously and raced to a breezy Individual century long before lunch, the like of which the Indore crowd had never seen before and which took them to heights of ecstasies.

No sooner had I swiped Gaekwad to fine leg boundary to hoist my century, I saw a multitude of enthusiastic fans invading the ground and, converging from all sides, they literally mobbed me. Everyone wanted to congratulate me personally, garland me, give presents-in cash and kind. They craved for handshakes and patted me rather too enthusiastically.

It was after quite some time that the crowd started melting away and when I was back to my senses after being thus mobbed, I felt that my pockets were overflowing with oranges, bananas, guavas and the like. As is customary in such situations, as also for better mobility, I emptied my pockets and handed over the sundry contents to the umpires; of course, let me confide, I preferred not to part with the paper currency which was also thrust in my pocket, in good measure, I was sure.

Back in my secluded room in the hotel that evening I settled to take stock of the cash that the crowd so voluntarily had put in my pockets as a token of their appreciation for my splendid display with the bat. Spontaneous exhibition of appreciation of crowd in the manner of invading the ground and making presents, big and small, are not unusual events and I had experienced such moments many a time in my cricketing career.

The bag of Rs 77, in various denominations of currency, therefore, was not much of a surprise, though I must confess this it was the biggest I had ever received on any occasion. But the presence of three lottery tickets did surprise me a great deal and I really wondered about the ingenuity of those who thought of making such a present.

Whatever charitable and noble purposes the lotteries must be serving, personally I have always been averse to it because of my belief that the prize money, if ever earned. cannot be termed as an earned Income and for that matter I have never gone in for a lottery ticket, its ever so Increasing popularity notwithstanding. But that's a purely personal matter.

Back home, after winding up our Ranji fixtures, I came across a news item in the newspapers a month later that the first prize winner of the Delhi State Lottery had not turned up to claim his prize and that a hot hunt was on for the lucky person. Further particulars revealed that the lucky ticket was sold to someone at Indore.

Not that I was in any way trying to piece up threads of wishful optimism but through simple, innocent inquisitiveness I soon found myself engaged in sorting out papers in my attaché, which I had carried along to Indore, in search of those lottery tickets which I had no mind to preserve except by reason of their being important mementoes of my memorable Innings.

Perhaps, if only I had known where I was heading to, I would certainly have refrained from embarking on my search, for, lo! and behold! one of the tickets did pertain to the Delhi State Lottery and bore exactly the same lucky number as given in the newspaper. No mistaking, to be sure.

Believe me, I have no words to describe the mental torture I underwent during the next three days. The seven-digit figure of Rs 11,00,000 prominently displayed across the lucky ticket, became part and parcel of my vision and moved around my eyes like the black spots, which revolve round a cataract patient's eyes, and then there was my own doctrine, of course, repugnant to the popular view, that the money earned through lotteries is not a properly earned income and, therefore, not acceptable to my religion.

Human weakness being what it is, the human element in me ultimately dominated. A bogged conscience left principles and doctrines to the four winds. I argued within, loosely though, that if I can accept Rs 77 and treat as principally valid then why not Rs 11 lakhs which has also been received in the same fashion. Well! The fact of the matter is that the windfall of Rs 11 lakhs was simply too much for any doctrines to stand in the way and I wasted no time in setting out for Delhi by the first available train to claim my prize and become a man of lakhs overnight.

The receptionist at the Ashoka Hotel guided me to the fifth floor and during the ascent in the lift I prepared myself for a stupendous welcome at the lotteries Office.

Vis-à-vis the officer at the table, to whom I presented the lucky ticket, I had a rude jolt when the glum faced creature failed to observe even the normal courtesy of offering me a chair. Instead, he cast a seemingly suspicious look at me from top to toe, pulled the side-drawers of his table searchingly, drew out a magnifying glass from within and hurriedly made a close examination of my ticket.

His manners, in my estimation, were far from worthy; nevertheless, I thought he was performing his duties.

His next move was, however, most alarming. Picking up the receiver of his telephone he dialled hastily. "Hello! Its lotteries office, Ashoka Hotel. Another case, Inspector! Could you come post haste?"

I could jolly well smell there was something fishy, though not quite exactly what. On replacing the receiver, the officer started showering questions at me. To start with he made out my descriptive roll. And then the meaningful question: "From where did you get this ticket"? I started narrating the whole story and while I was doing so a police Inspector entered in and started the questioning again from the scratch.

My replies must have been straight forward and to the point because I noticed that both the officials in turn started questioning as if they were interrogating a suspect criminal but as they progressed there was a marked softening in their tone and temper. Finally, the police Inspector very politely explained to me that the lucky ticket presented by me was a fake one and the police was apprehensive that a well organised gang of cheats have engaged themselves in forging lottery tickets. Apologising, he continued, that he was afraid he would have to detain me till investigations in this respect were complete.

It hardly warrants a mention that what had transpired from the time I had presented my lucky (rather unlucky) ticket was too unnerving and I was all but in tears. I felt extremely panicky particularly on hearing the word 'detention' and pleaded rather nervously that I be allowed to go as being a Central Government employee my detention here might adversely affect my official career. In response, they tried to discount my apprehensions, yet couldn't accede to my requests. In an obvious effort to buck me up they tried to comfort me by elucidating the term 'detention' as nothing more than my compulsorily accepting their 'hospitality' for a few days at the Ashoka Hotel.

I had no option but to act according to their dictates and I was shown to a posh room on the third floor.

The very thought of a relief, temporary though, from the presence of those two interrogating officers was most welcome. But by any stretch of imagination, I could not even dream of the situation I was about to confront.

Realising that I had, perhaps, been inadvertently shown into a wrong room I hastily apologized *'I beg your pardon'* and retreated as I saw the lonely occupant of that thickly curtained and lavishly furnished room a beautiful damsel, lying in the only bed, taken by surprise on my sudden entry. The sentry at the door, who had escorted me, removed whatever doubts I had in no uncertain terms and advised me, politely, I must say, that I should make no attempt to escape (as if I was making one, eh!).

Introducing myself to the beautiful lady, gorgeously dressed, who had by now risen, but still in bed, I explained to her briefly the circumstances under which I was thrust in and that I was not trespassing by any chance.

Contrary to my expectations, the lady seemed to be mightily relieved by my arrival and she made no secret of her feelings while narrating, in a very sweet voice, her own tale that landed her there.

Though absolute strangers, we were thick and thin in incredibly short time. And why not? Were we not sailing in the same boat? Her story also was almost identical to mine as she had also presented at the lottery office a ticket bearing the lucky number.

Incidentally, she had also got possession of the ticket in the similar fashion as I had though in a different field in which she excelled.

Hours passed and we talked ceaselessly, in the process acquainting ourselves very closely, and the more we knew about each other, the more we seem to be fascinated and attached to each other. She hailed from Bombay and was a great exponent of Kathak dance. She had to her credit performances at all the Important centers of India and it was during one such performance at Indore that she had received the disputed lottery ticket, along with other presents, in cash and kind, in appreciation of her display by some connoisseur of art.

Being myself a passionate lover of classical music and dance she became my instant heroine and, to cap it all, when I learnt that, after dancing, cricket was her first craze, there was no limit of my fascination for her. What a subtle and fine knowledge of cricket she had, I wondered if most of our present-day cricketers are in the know of. Mind you, she rated Stanley Mc Cabe as a cricketing giant even though a contemporary of Bradman; considered Douglas Jardine, and not Harold Larwood, responsible for 'bodyline' controversy: regarded Peter May as the pioneer of on-side play; thought running between the wickets an art: wished she could see Colin Bland's fielding; was sorry for Collie Smith's and Amar Singh's premature deaths; loved reading Neville Cardus and Ray Robinson, etc., etc.

And then she seemed to be filled with joy while listening with rapt attention about my interest and depth of understanding of the finer points of music and dancing. It was fascinating for her to learn that I was a prize winner in the junior section of the competitions in the 1945 Music Conference at Allahabad and had given a violin recital before Alauddin Khan. She raised her eyebrows in wonder when I commented that Bandana Sen's bhavana and expressions of lips and eyes were by far the most promising; that I longed to see Uday 'Shankar's 'Kalpana' again and again; considered Birjoo Maharaj's Sham-e-Oudh' an essay in the classical mould; was full of admiration for Miss Jayakar's novelties in modern dance but was sorry not to hear her name; rated Sitara Devi a class in herself; and could appreciate Gopi Krishna's novel presentation of laikari while delivering speech simultaneously.

It was past mid-night and both of us were feeling it was time we went to bed. I had stretched myself on the sofa but despite the heater in the corner, the biting cold of January did require a blanket. There was no way out, however, It was a single seated room and, therefore, furnished with one bed only.

What an understanding lady she was. After about half an hour of our deciding to sleep, during which time I am sure she must have debated at length mentally, she proposed with her voice full of maturity that since we both were victims of unforeseen, unexpected circumstances and in view of the bitter cold, I might share the bed with her, if I so preferred.

I must frankly confess that the offer, coming as it was from her end, was the least expected and I was mightily surprised. But then was it not a day of surprises and unexpected happenings?

Expressing my sincere gratitudes I rose up, put off the lights, lighted the night bulb and slipped into the warm, cosy bed.

Very warm bed, indeed.

No words were exchanged. Perfect calm and tranquillity prevailed. I did not know about her, but so far as I was concerned, I was feigning fast asleep although wide awake. I was unable to account for my restlessness even though so comfortably placed.

As time passed the state of my restlessness was turning into unbearable agony and at length, I wonder what prompted me to turn towards her and whisper to enquire if she was awake.

She was!

I am sure if I had tried to gather courage and understood what I was about to say, perhaps, I would not have uttered. Rather bluntly, I stammered, *"Can I, can I treat you as my wife?"*

When she looked at me. I realised what a blunder I had committed. But no, perhaps, not. With eyes feigning to be sleepy she graciously acquiesced "As you like".

Well, in keeping with the trend of strange happenings that day, I promptly said "Thank you", turned to other side and started snoring soon after.

I don't think I snore in sleep; at least none has ever complained and I understand it is only the bulky people who snore.

But that night I must really have snored, and snored quite loudly for, being a light-sleeper, I was awakened by the sheer noise of my snoring to find myself in a cosy bed in a hotel at Indore with my plastered right hand heavily resting on my chest.

Well, funny nightmare, wasn't that? Freud held that while asleep one's mind is like a boat in a river, one end of which is the past; the other, the future. When the boat sails towards the 'past' end, dreams depict happenings of the past; and when it sails towards 'future', coming events show themselves in some form.

Whatever be the truth, the entire sequence of events were replete with incongruous absurdities. I never played in the match described because of an injury sustained at the 'trials' at Varanasi. The injury lingered, and a day before the Ranji fixture at Indore in 1957-58, my hand was put in plaster after an X-Ray in the Gandhi Hospital, Indore. Secondly, the lotteries are of comparatively recent origin and even if they were in vogue in late 'fifties', never were such fabulous prizes offered.

And finally, for the information of those astute readers who may appreciate its relevancy here, I was not even married then!!